BEGIN AGAIN

END DAYS BOOK 4

EE ISHERWOOD
CRAIG MARTELLE

CONNECT WITH CRAIG MARTELLE

Website & Newsletter:
www.craigmartelle.com

BookBub –
www.bookbub.com/authors/craig-martelle

Facebook:
www.facebook.com/AuthorCraigMartelle/

CONNECT WITH E.E. ISHERWOOD

Website & Newsletter:
www.sincethesirens.com

Facebook:
facebook.com/sincethesirens

Cover Illustration by Heather Hamilton-Senter
Editing services provided by Lynne Stiegler
Formatting by James Osiris Baldwin – jamesosiris.com

We couldn't do what we do without the support of great people around us. We thank our spouses and our families for giving us time alone to think, write, and review. We thank our editor (Lynne), cover artist (Heather), and insider team of beta readers (Micky Cocker, Kelly O'Donnell, Dr. James Caplan, and John Ashmore). It's not who we are as authors, but who we are surrounded by that makes this all happen. Enjoy the story.

ONE

Sidney, NE

"You're awake, aren't you?" Connie asked.

Buck shifted in the Peterbilt's sleeper. "Yeah. How could you tell?"

At some point in the night, Mac had hopped off the bed, so he and Connie could have spread out a little. However, instead of using the extra space, the dog's absence had made them move closer together. Now she was huddled against his chest, probably because she was always cold in the air-conditioned sleeper cab.

"Your breathing changed when you woke up. Thinking about Garth?"

He glanced at the digital clock next to the bed. The dim red LED numbers showed 4:44 in the morning. He'd gotten a few hours of sleep, which he desperately needed, but he had been up for a while already, stewing about what might have prevented Garth from calling him.

"Garth. The world. Our convoy. You. Everything. I've been trying to pretend what's going on outside is temporary, and that once we get to Garth things are going to return to the way they were, but I'm coming to terms with the truth. This is Day Four, and those scientists still aren't saying shit about fixing things. Nothing is going back to the way it was."

Connie reached out in the darkness and draped her arm over his neck as if to hold him where she wanted him. "I've been thinking about my boy, too. He was in a dream of mine, in fact."

"A good one, I hope," Buck remarked.

"Not really. I haven't had a good dream since I came to 2020. Well, there was that one time where I had a daydream about you and me..." She chuckled mischievously.

"I'm listening," Buck replied with great interest.

"Oh, I shouldn't have teased you at a time like this. It's just I hate thinking bad thoughts, and that's all my dreams seem to be about. Phillip is always fighting Saddam Hussein in a swirling sandstorm, so I never know if he makes it out of there alive."

He wanted to hear more about her pleasant dream, but family always came first.

"I told you, we kicked Saddam and his army right in the nuts. It's all good. You shouldn't worry about that."

"Maybe you're right. My maternal instincts are screaming that he has to be alive, but my tired brain has me convinced it is just the opposite."

"Go with the maternal side," he suggested.

"I try to, every moment I'm awake. There are times when I'm positive I sense him nearby, but it's probably wishful thinking. Do you feel your son's presence across the miles?"

He laughed. "I've never stopped feeling a connection to him. From the day he was born, and no matter how many miles away from home I go, I always sense him. I even convinced myself I knew when he was getting into trouble, and I would sometimes call his friend Sam's parents to check on him, but I stopped doing that when I figured out my Spidey senses weren't as great as I thought. The reality was, he *always* got into trouble with that boy."

She laughed sympathetically, then continued speaking. "Well, I know we're all in trouble with this time-travel shit, but my nightmares felt more vivid last night. I want to believe he is close."

"You want to try calling him, don't you?" Buck pointed to his phone on the charger nearby. "I won't lie, Connie. I've been thinking about ringing Garth no matter what the hour, too. Let's get out of bed and hit the phone together."

She kept her arm over his neck a little longer.

"Thank you, Buck. For everything. The ride. A place to stay. A friend in a land I barely understand. It's been an effort to hold it together. I tear up at odd times, and for no apparent reason. I can't imagine where I'd be if I had to do this alone. Finding my son will, I think, go a long way toward fighting off the waterworks forever."

"You're welcome. You've complained about yourself before, but I've seen nothing but strength from you. You're killing it in my timeline."

"I don't like to be the weeping damsel in distress. I'm not that type."

He gripped her hand tightly. "No one would ever mistake you for a pushover, Connie. Besides, I have a good feeling about today. We're going to reach Garth—I'm sure of that. Then we're going to find your boy. He's out there, too. If he's your son, he has to be a survivor."

For the millionth time, Buck considered kissing her, but he didn't want to ruin the tender moment. After waiting to see if she would say anything more, he hopped out of bed and put on his guns-and-grenades Hawaiian shirt.

"You don't have anything else to wear?" she taunted.

"I washed this in the Great Salt Lake yesterday." It smelled of salt water, but at least it wasn't rank with sweat. "And I can't get my maid to come in and do the laundry."

"Yeah, well, I know a Marine who buys me new clothes when my old ones get wet and dirty."

"Sounds like an awesome dude." His words could have come out of Garth's mouth. That boy and his friends all talked like surfers for some reason.

"Maybe. I'm still not sure about him..." She left the words hanging. The day needed to start.

"Want a water?" he asked, deliberately looking away from her. There were a few bottles in the mini-fridge. As he pulled one out, he remembered he'd stuffed the rabbit into the freezer section.

I've got to cook it soon.

"Nah, I'll get something stronger when we go into the truck stop for breakfast."

"Suit yerself," he drawled.

He got situated in the driver's seat as she slid into the passenger position. After a quick glance at his dash lights to make sure there were no problems, he turned to her. She, however, stared out the window.

"It's amazing," she said with awe.

The eastern horizon was aglow with the first hints of dawn, but the nighttime sky above was filled with translucent ribbons of green, purple, and yellow. The wavy shimmers of energy nearly filled the entire sky. Even the lights of the truck stop couldn't wash out the beautiful swipes of color hanging up there.

"That's a new one," he deadpanned.

Connie craned her neck to look out the windshield. "Is that the aurora borealis?"

"Maybe. I've seen hints of the aurora in some of the northern states, but I've never seen anything even close to this. The colors are incredible."

"The atmosphere must be really messed up," Connie suggested.

He absently turned on the radio, thinking the news might have something about it, but Mac nudged his leg before he could tune in.

"I've got to take him outside. I guess we're all waking up." He had hoped the pup would sleep in for a few more minutes.

"I'll call the other trucks," she replied. "Get everyone up and ready to roll out. That's what you want, isn't it?"

He smiled at her. "That is exactly what I want. The faster we run off some miles, the sooner we'll reach Garth."

She reached over and put her hand on his thigh. "Buck, we will find your son. If he's anything like you, he's resourceful and strong. The energy waves may have made you black out a little, but they didn't stop you, and I'm positive they didn't stop him either. Bank on it."

He didn't feel great, but he did feel better.

It was time to get back on the road.

Charleston, WV

Garth's body shifted like he'd been tossed out a window.

"What the..." he blurted, grasping for the steering wheel. His heart pounded in his chest like a time bomb set to explode.

He found himself in the front seat of the taxi, although it took a full second to realize it wasn't moving. As he caught his breath, it became obvious he'd startled himself awake from a heavy slumber.

"Are you okay?" Lydia asked with concern from the back seat.

"Oh, yeah," he replied, ordering his heart to defuse itself. "I dreamed I was falling. That's all."

Lydia laughed quietly. "Sometimes wagon drivers would tumble to the ground when they fell asleep during the day. It made children burst out laughing. Pa never did that, but I did see him doze off now and then."

"That was why I pulled into this campground last night," he replied. "I almost conked out a few times while I was driving, because I was exhausted. When my body fought off the sleep, it was like what I just experienced. It felt like falling."

"How do you feel now? You didn't get much sleep, but the sun is up now so we can continue."

He sighed with a heavy heart. The sun poked through the trees of the campground, but it was only a few minutes past six. If he'd been at home, he could have easily gone back to bed and not woke up until noon. By contrast, the hardworking pioneer girl had been awake before him both mornings.

"We made good time last night. I set the odometer on this car. We did almost five hundred miles. I was also able to stop at another gas station and filled up the whole tank. I don't think we'll have to use the two-gallon container again."

"You didn't wake me up at the station?" she asked with surprise.

"I wanted to let you sleep. Besides, there were no other cars there, so we didn't have any threats to worry about."

Since he'd lost his pistol, the only defensive gun he had left was one of the AR-15s he kept in the gun case. He didn't want to carry it around, however. He'd never seen his dad carry a rifle around town, and he figured he should follow the same rules. He was already inside a stolen taxi, although he'd painted the outside black to hide all the markings. Doing things at night, when there were few people, suited him just fine.

"You missed a beautiful light show in the sky, though. I almost woke you up to see it, but I figured you probably saw the northern lights all the time since you lived under the stars."

"I would have enjoyed seeing it with you," she admitted, "but I understand your reasoning. We must both get our rest so we can function inside this tack-see today."

"Agreed. And lucky for us, we don't have a tent to break down." Last night, he'd pulled into the little KOA campground to save money, instead of getting a room in a motel. However, after he'd paid for a spot and driven the final fifty yards, he'd had no energy to get out and set up a tent, so they'd slept in the car.

"What time is it?" Lydia asked.

"A little after six in the morning. I guess I got an hour and a half of sleep." He said it while hiding the disappointment he felt. If he was going to drive all day, which was his plan, he wasn't sure ninety minutes of sleep was enough.

"Garth, we aren't alone here."

He peered out his empty window frame.

"Oh, shit. I pulled into the wrong space."

It was easy to see what happened. He'd parked alongside another campsite instead of pulling into the one he'd been assigned. Now, a man and woman broke down their tent just a few feet outside his window.

The woman caught his eye. "Sorry, dear, we need you to move as soon as you can. We have to back out."

He felt like an idiot. Not only had he parked outside his own spot, but he'd blocked the neighbor campers into theirs.

"Sorry," he said in a low voice. "I was pretty tired last night when I got here."

"We heard you come in," she responded while pulling apart tent poles.

The couple were in their forties or fifties—older than his dad, but not old people. They were dressed in high-priced clothing like they had some money. He recognized the North Face windbreaker worn by the man as clothing the rich kids at school liked to wear.

"Where you heading?" he asked.

"Denver," she replied. "It's where the internet said to go, right?"

The man shushed his wife.

She shushed him back. "We have to be polite, babe."

"I know, babe, but we don't want the *whole* world to go there, you know?"

The woman turned back to Garth, apparently undeterred. "That man on the videos said the SNAKE lab was the only safe place in America, so that's where we're going. You should go there too."

"Denver?" Garth responded. He recalled his dad telling him to avoid that city, but he didn't volunteer the information, because he didn't know if something had changed. "I'm not going that far, but I am driving out west to meet my dad. We'll probably go back to New York once we link up. First, though, I need to find a phone and call him to find out where he is."

The woman pulled out a phone. "You can use mine."

He felt elated to have the opportunity, but that faded with the speed of a shooting star. "Thanks, but I don't know his number. We're going to the first mall we find to look up his information at my cell phone company."

She tapped the phone and made like she was going to talk on it, but then she gave it an odd glance. "The network is down? It was working fine last night."

The woman shrugged. "I was going to dial information for you. They might know his listing."

"That only works for local numbers, babe," her husband said from inside the deflating tent.

She looked at her partner for a few seconds, then put her phone away. "I guess we'll never know. Going to the cell phone company sounds smart. I wish you the best of luck." She continued in a quieter voice, so her husband wouldn't hear. "And you should consider going to Denver. I bet most people in this campground are going there. You don't want to be late."

"Late?" he asked in the same tone. "Late for what?"

"The end of it all. End Times. The last page of human history. Aren't you following in the news on the internet?"

Garth's anxiety came roaring back. If she was right and everyone at the campground was going west, he felt a compulsion to get a head start on them.

"I am following it, yes. Thanks, and good luck."

He started the car.

"Lydia, come on up to the front seat. I need you to keep me from falling asleep. We're good on gas, but we're going to make one unscheduled stop."

She scrambled out of the car and got into the passenger seat.

"What do we need, Garth?"

"Lots and lots of Mountain Dew. We aren't stopping until I reach my dad."

TWO

***Search for Nuclear, Astrophysical, and Krono-
metric Extremes (SNAKE). Red Mesa, Colorado***

Faith was roused from her fitful sleep by engine noises outside.

"What now?"

She'd spent the night across the hall from her old office. Now that General Smith was dead, she could probably take it over again, except that all the windows were broken. She had gone in there to get a look at the heavy machinery on the parking lot, although she thought twice about it when her feet crunched on glass.

The sunrise over the high plains of Colorado shone in through the empty window frames, and it reflected off millions of shards of glass on the floor, on her desk, and on all the shelves and cabinets. The car bomb had knocked down all her knickknacks, thrown her computer on the floor, and punched out most of the ceiling tiles.

The only thing missing from the crime scene was a long strand of yellow police tape.

While staying low to avoid being seen, she peeked outside.

"Is this the help you said was coming?" she muttered sadly, thinking again of Smith.

Several tanks scooted around the parking lot like roaches through the woodwork. These were real tanks, not the Humvees she had seen the day before. Huge guns poked out of the turrets of the tracked monsters making them appear far more menacing up close.

On the far side of the parking lot, beefy military tractors shoved civilian cars into the brush.

"Assholes!"

Her Jeep was somewhere on that side.

"There better be a damned good explanation for this!" she grumbled as she walked into the hallway.

Bob ran into the office where she'd spent the night.

"Hey, Bob. I'm over here."

He popped his head back out and smiled a little when he saw her. "There you are. We have to get out of here. More soldiers are arriving, and they're trying to round us up again."

She took it in stride. "The military was already here. NORAD, remember?"

"Yeah, but these guys have lots of guns, and they aren't fucking around like last time. Faith, they're being rough with our people. I don't think they're going to let anyone leave. That's why we have to go." He waited for a second, as if unsure what she was going to do. "Right now!"

"Yeah, okay," she allowed.

They jogged down the hallway toward one of the many emergency exits. Because the SNAKE facility was almost entirely underground, the designers had been overly cautious about providing exit routes. She'd used one of them last night to escape the collider tunnel after the explosion, and now they were going to save her again.

"Where will we go?" She thought of her Jeep being tossed around outside. "I don't know what they're thinking, but the first thing they did was shovel my Jeep off the parking lot."

"My Audi is probably scrap now too. We'll worry about that when we get outside. Come on!"

Screams echoed from other hallways, and she expected Army men to appear around every corner, but they made it to a metal door with the EXIT sign above it. Bob went through and held it open, but she stopped at the threshold.

"We have to help others escape," she said urgently. There weren't any other scientists close by, but there were some milling around down the hall.

"Faith, listen to me. The NORAD security guards are gone. They were chased away. I've been trying to tell you. These new guys aren't going to be as accommodating as General Smith. They might even be here to punish us."

She squinted at him as if he'd just told a huge fib. "Come on, the military doesn't do that. General Smith was very clear about their role."

"Yeah, and you said he was bringing in the people responsible for the experiment. What if they couldn't find them? What if the military got sick of the whole waiting game and they're just going to eliminate the people who know mistakes were made?"

Faith saw beyond his words. "And since you were part of the group that started this whole disaster, you think they are out for you, right?"

"Believe me, I only knew what little I needed to run the

experiment, but there are multiple levels of the military, Faith. The grunts who kick in doors and the generals who tell them what to do, and then there are the eggheads who design and test the superweapons."

"That's still not—"

He continued, "Then there are the bosses who decide which superweapons get made and which ones get scrapped. If they are scrapping this, we all might be collateral damage."

"That's a lot of ifs."

Bob propped open the door as wide as it would go. "I'm leaving, Faith. I want you to go as well. They have tanks and guns. I want nothing to do with all that."

She walked through the door as if she were in a dream. Deep down she didn't believe any bad could come from having the military around, but she had to admit that General Smith might have spoiled her with his straightforward honesty. These new soldiers had tanks, guns, and bulldozers, and didn't seem to have any problem flaunting them.

They killed my Jeep!

General Smith's people never would have done that.

"Come on. Hurry!" He started up the stairwell, waited for a second to see if she would follow, and then kept going.

The main administration wing of SNAKE was built into solid rock, as was the rest of the facility, but there wasn't much earth above it because it was near the surface. They had three or four flights before reaching the exterior door leading out into the forest.

Screams floated up from the lab below, like her people were being hurt as they were rounded up.

"This doesn't feel right," she said with uncertainty. "We could have gotten some of them out with us."

Bob seemed to ignore her. "I'm leaving through this door and heading to freedom. You need to come with me right now."

Faith took a step back. "I was able to negotiate with General Smith. I helped prevent a disaster by stopping him from shutting down the Four Arrows boxes at the same time. What if I leave and no one is there to stop the next calamity?"

"You can't be sure that's what will happen. There's only one box left. Whatever they screw up, we have to be far away from here when it happens."

"No, I've changed my mind. I'm not going." She said it with all the bravado she was able to muster.

Bob pressed the latch of the fire door and chuckled. "I'm surprised I got you this close to freedom, actually. You care too much about your work. I can see now that you did deserve the lead role more than I did."

He offered his hand, which she shook briefly.

"Take care of yourself, Faith, okay? I won't go far, I promise. I might talk to some colleagues up in Boulder and get a better read on what's going on outside of SNAKE. Sound good?"

"I suppose. Don't think we're done, though. You owe me an explanation for how you set up this illegal experiment in the first place, but for now, I hope you get to safety. It can't hurt to have allies on the outside."

He looked surprised. "You consider me an ally? After all I've done to you?"

She ran her fingers through her hair, surprised at herself for having used the word.

"For now, let's just agree we have the same enemies, okay? Being my ally will depend on what you share with me, got it?"

"Deal," he agreed with his usual smug look.

He pushed through the door, but when he turned to go outside, something slapped his face. Bob's head was flung back, and blood splattered on the door, and on her blouse.

He crumpled to the concrete a second later.

I-80, NE

Buck and his convoy were back on the interstate. Sparky had tipped over his truck last night, so he rode with Eve, the trucking recruiter. Mel "Monsignor" Tinker drove the third truck and stayed far at the back. He preferred to be alone with his flammable tanker because he was terrified he was going to blow up with it.

"Sure is pretty," Connie remarked, looking forward. The sun crept up over the flat prairie of high plains Nebraska.

"Don't let it fool you," he shot back. "You're going to get sick of this state before you know it."

She chuckled. "I'm already sick of it, but I'm trying my best to pretend. Otherwise, I might start asking you if we're there yet. My boy was a master at making trips like this seem like an eternity. It was murder getting him to be quiet and read a book."

Buck turned her way. "You would like having a kid today. All you have to do is give them a digital tablet, and it babysits them for the entire trip. You have to struggle to get them to put it down so you can feed them."

Connie expressed disgust. "That sounds horrible. I don't want some gadget watching my son."

"Amen, sister," he replied, "but that's the way of the world. Garth plays games on his phone all the time. Sometimes I think about taking it away from him so he has to talk to his friends with a standard telephone, but that's a hard battle to wage when I'm always out on the road. I did manage to lay down the law so he can't play games during the school week."

He sighed.

"I should have been there more."

Connie grabbed his phone out of the cradle. She'd tried to call both of their sons once since they hit the highway, but she hit redial on Garth again.

"Buck, I promise you we'll get in touch with him, and eventually we'll get you two back together. Then you can tell him whatever you want. In person."

He waited while the phone rang. It went to voicemail, which he took as a good omen. At least it was connecting with something on the outside.

She handed him the phone.

"Hey, Garth. It's Dad. We're on our way to meet you, but we need to know where you are, like we discussed, so we can meet up. Call me as soon as you get this. Love you. Talk soon."

He hung up, and she started to dial again.

"Phil?" he inquired.

She nodded. "I can't stop trying. I'm sure he's out there."

"Come on, boys," he said with determination. "Pick up for your parents."

The phone rang over and over as he put more miles on his Peterbilt.

On the horizon far ahead, the sky went from light blue to thunderstorm green in a split second, but it wasn't a typical weather front. It was as if a storm had been teleported into existence with the snap of a god's fingers.

A strong gust of wind bashed against the front windshield like a shockwave from an explosion.

"Hang that up. We've got trouble."

He didn't want the distraction of a ringing phone.

The darkness of the storm spread out on both sides of the center point.

And it was getting closer.

Red Mesa, CO

Phil took charge of the three NORAD airmen because he outranked them, but they seemed anxious to have the leadership. They'd been run ragged since they drove to SNAKE from Peterson Air Force Base, and they didn't have nearly enough guards to watch over the entire facility. That was how the terrorists with backpacks of C-4 had been able to walk in and push them out the door into the woods.

"Sir, it looks like every exit is being watched now. We saw some scientists try to escape, and one of the guards used the butt of his rifle to break the guy's face."

Overnight, Phil and the three airmen had crept through the hilly forest until they reached the main offices of SNAKE. From their vantage point above the facility, they had a good view of the parking lot, the main office, and some of the concrete bunkers that served as exit doors.

For most of the night, Phil had been convinced he was part of an elaborate prank to make him think he'd been transported across the world in one second. However, when the sun came up and he saw the flat expanse of the city of Denver, he grudgingly admitted he wasn't in Switzerland anymore.

"Why would they hurt the scientists?" he asked his men.

Private Sanchez replied. "I don't know, sir, but if I did that to a civvy, I would expect to get court-martialed in half a second. The man wasn't a threat. They struck him for the hell of it as he walked through a door."

"I don't suppose any of you have radios?" he asked without much hope.

"We left one in the tunnels," Sanchez answered. "The terrorist wouldn't let us take weapons or anything else."

Phil's radioman, Corporal Barry Grafton, had last been seen in Geneva, Switzerland. He had no idea if any of his men had come to Colorado with him, but he was beginning to think he was going to have to scour the forest looking for them.

He pulled out his disposable phone, intending to call the Ranger headquarters at Fort Benning, but the phone was completely dead. The LED screen was blank.

"Son of a bitch," he groused. "I know this was charged when I left on our mission. Something depleted it."

"Maybe it was the trip from Switzerland," one of the men joked.

Phil didn't bother arguing. It might have been true.

He was about to ask if any of the three airmen carried personal phones, but the sounds of footfalls and low voices came from behind them.

"Shit!" he hissed. "Find cover." He was the only one with a weapon, so he tried to position himself between the voices and the unarmed guards. A tall pine provided a good hiding spot.

Phil caught glimpses of military uniforms through the pine saplings around the trail. Approximately four men, all armed.

He had about five seconds to decide if all of this was real. If this was America, the units had to be friendly. That meant pulling a gun on them could possibly be career-ending.

Yet, he was still on his original mission. In that respect, he had a duty to avoid capture until he understood what happened to Ethan and the rest of his unit.

This is America, dammit. It has to be.

THREE

I-80, NE

"What's going on out there?" Monsignor asked over the CB. "Another storm?"

Buck peered ahead, not sure what it was. The darkness was like an infection inside the baby blue of the normal sky. The sun was blotted out by part of the anomaly, but it wasn't because of any clouds.

A chill clung to his spine from the base of his skull to the middle of his back.

He let off the gas a little.

"It isn't a storm," Connie said with fear in her voice. He watched as she reached down to pet Mac, and she seemed surprised when he wasn't there.

"He's in his crate," he said after seeing her look around.

"I don't blame him. I also feel like curling up back in bed," she replied. "I don't know why."

Buck got on the CB. "It doesn't matter what it is. We're going to punch through it."

"I'm behind you, Buck," Eve responded. "Sparky says he agrees with you."

Buck drove for a few more miles as he studied the roadway ahead. A fine mist forced him to flip on his windshield wipers, although there were still no clouds ahead.

"There!" Connie declared. "What's that?"

She pointed to a building next to the highway a few miles down the road. There were no cities in this part of Nebraska, so he guessed it was a large grain silo, but he soon crossed that off the list because the shape was completely wrong.

"It looks like a skyscraper lying on its side," he replied.

"This feels wrong," he said slow and mechanically, "like the darkness doesn't belong here. That shouldn't be here." He pointed to the huge monotone gray structure.

Buck strained to decipher what it was as he drove the lonely interstate through the grasslands. They were a mile from the structure when the grass changed, almost as if he'd crossed a property line. On one side it was green and healthy. On the far side, closer to the object, the grass had been stripped away and replaced with mud. An intense rain had scoured away grass and clawed ditches down the small, rolling hills, and pools of water gathered in every low point.

"Oh, hell, no. It can't be." Buck was close enough to the shape to recognize the lines and the proportions.

"You know what it is?" Connie asked.

He waited another twenty seconds as they came alongside the mystery object.

"Buck?" she pressed.

"Yes. It's a ship. An aircraft carrier, to be precise."

"Here?" she said with surprise. "In Nebraska? That's impossible."

"I'm positive that's what it is, and I don't think the locals built it as a tourist attraction."

The eerie atmosphere seemed to dissipate as they

approached, a lot like a fog that went away when they were inside it. As they got closer, the shape came into focus, and he was certain what it was. He figured the darkness was because of the evaporating water around the ship. The hull of the metallic beast was also soaked, like it had been pulled from the ocean and dropped in Nebraska as part of a giant claw-grab arcade game.

Sparky spoke on the CB. "Buck, do I need to get my eyes checked? Did that ship sail over a thousand miles of farmland to get out here?"

He picked up the handset but took a moment to think about it. "We've seen storms pop out of nowhere. We've heard of planes and people coming from the past. It looks like bigger things are coming through now."

The ship's hull was covered in barnacles and sea slime, but it was also crumpled and damaged as if it had been dropped into position alongside the highway. It wasn't a modern American aircraft carrier, he knew that much, but he had no idea where or when it might have come from.

"Aw shit, here we go again," he said when the traffic jam became apparent. "Gawkers. We can't avoid them. There are almost no cars for a hundred miles either way on the interstate, but when we get to crap like this, there is nothing but rubberneckers."

Connie laughed. "Maybe they came out of the past too? What if these people were plucked from traffic jams in Los Angeles or New York City? Wouldn't they be surprised to end up in Nebraska with this ship to look at?"

Buck engaged the Jakes and slowed the Peterbilt to a crawl. There were maybe fifty cars and trucks pulled over on both sides of the highway. Lots of people were on foot, taking pictures.

"Can we get out and look at it?" Eve requested. "I

would love to get some video for my promotional material. Truckers see some of the most interesting shit on the road, that's for sure."

He didn't know if he really wanted to indulge the young woman, but this was a once-in-a-lifetime opportunity.

"Mac does need to get out and do his business." Connie spoke as if she knew he was thinking about stopping.

Buck motioned to the phone. "Try Garth one more time, please. If he doesn't pick up, I might need to run around outside the truck to blow off some of this tension."

"Oh, good. I'll tie the leash to your belt, and you can exercise Big Mac."

The Golden Retriever barked when he heard his name.

"See?" she went on. "He's game."

"I don't know..."

Connie reached out to him, causing an electrical shock between her fingertips and his knee. "We're making good time. We've been on the road for two hours, and we have an excuse to stop. The other drivers could use a break."

That was all he needed to make his decision.

"Okay, folks," he said over the CB, "we're going to pull over and check this out. We're not staying long, so get out and stretch. Eat a snack. I need you refreshed so we can keep piling on these miles. My son is counting on me to get to him, and our customers are still expecting their deliveries."

"Roger that," Sparky replied.

"Thanks, Dad," Eve said with a giggle.

"Don't make me come back there, young lady. I'll turn this whole convoy around if I have to."

Buck turned to Connie to find her smiling.

"What? Am I being too goofy?"

"No, not at all. I was terrified again when we first saw

23

this thing." She pointed to the ship looming above them about a hundred yards to the left of the highway. "Now I feel like we're all in this together. It doesn't scare me."

"I'm not scared either," he fibbed.

No matter what other problems he faced getting back to Garth, he now had to worry about ships dropping from the sky. Someday in the future, he'd look back and laugh, but today, the only thing he could do was revel in the absurdity of it all.

Louisville, KY

Garth knew things were going to be okay the instant he saw the sign for the shopping mall.

"It says the mall is open!" he remarked to Lydia. He pointed to the digital billboard next to the highway. "I was beginning to wonder if they had closed on account of all the problems."

"That's amazing," she replied. "How does the sign know?"

He was taken aback. Garth wasn't sure of the science behind it, but it was like anything else in the world of technology. It just worked.

"When the mall is open, the sign changes so it shows as open. When they close, the sign will say it's closed."

"Incredible," she gushed.

He exited the highway onto a side road. A few minutes later, they pulled into a parking spot at the giant mall, and her amazement ran wild.

"I've never seen a place so big. This is all one store?"

"You won't believe it. Come on!" He got out of the taxi and walked to the trunk. He briefly considered that he was unarmed and at the mercy of the people inside the mall to behave, but he still wasn't prepared to carry a rifle. After the slight delay, he rushed around to help her out.

"Thank you, Garth. You are a gentleman." She smiled happily.

Her words made him feel important.

Garth beamed as they walked hand in hand through the front doors of the mall. Lydia was less impressed with the auto-doors this time, but she was blown away when she saw the inside of the building.

"You put a whole town inside!" She let go of his hand, pulled off her bonnet, and looked down the rows of stores.

"That's true," he replied. Seen through her eyes, the shopping mall was another modern marvel, but his interest in the place was based on the disaster outside. He couldn't help but notice that about half the stores still had their metal gates blocking the entrances.

"Come on," he advised. "We have to keep moving."

A few of the gates rose as they walked as if the mall had just opened, but many remained down. People milled about some of those gates, waiting for them to open. The closed gate for the video game store had the most people in front of it, although he didn't understand why.

"We have to find a kiosk, Lydia. It isn't a store, but more like a cart that hangs out in the middle of the mall. I've seen them at a couple of malls back in New York. I hope they have them here, too."

"You don't know for sure?" she asked.

Before he could reply, a man in gym shorts and a t-shirt ran between him and Lydia like he was doing the fifty-yard dash. The guy elbowed Garth in the hip as he flew by.

"Shit!" Garth spat.

A second man dressed the same way trailed the first by two seconds. He didn't run between them, but Garth had

25

jumped aside after the first guy, so the other man had to push him out of the way too.

"Damn!" he yelled.

He turned back to Lydia, then noticed another runner. An African-American in a blue Security uniform turned a corner and appeared to look for the escaping runners.

"Hey!" Garth shouted as he pointed where the two men had gone. "They went that way!"

The guard sprinted by. "Thanks!"

Other shoppers stood around watching the spectacle with expressions Garth recognized immediately. He'd seen it on the subway. On the streets of New York. At La Guardia airport.

He whispered. "C'mon. We have to hurry. They opened the mall, but maybe not for long."

Far down the row of stores, opposite of where the guard had gone, another man jogged with a huge box in his arms.

Garth went to grab Lydia's hand, but a woman ran into him.

"Oof," he exhaled. "I feel like I'm in a fucking bumper car!"

The woman dropped a plastic shopping bag, and a few toys fell to the tiled floor.

"Oh, shit, I'm sorry, miss!" he said as he bent over to help pick up.

The woman was maybe in her twenties. She was plain, with short black hair and battleship-gray eyes. She wore jeans and a faded black t-shirt with a beer logo on the front.

The woman grabbed for the fallen toys. "I need my stuff, man. Help me pick it up." Her accent was distinctly Southern.

Garth handed her a silver-colored cowboy pistol. He

couldn't see what else was in the bag, but he bet a kid's silver sheriff star was in there to go with the gun.

"I'm really sorry. I didn't mean to knock your, uh, stuff out of the bag."

The woman looked up at him once she had the gun in the bag again, but she turned to the nearest wall. "Do you see them? They're inside all the brickwork. They buzz. They listen. They're just waiting for the signal to come out."

Garth got back to his feet, unsure what to say.

"What are they?" Lydia asked, drawn into the discussion.

The dark-haired woman seemed to notice her for the first time. "You. You don't belong." She hopped onto her feet and stumbled back a few paces. "You aren't from here, either. Just like them." She pointed to the wall again.

Garth thought that was hilarious. Lydia was dressed like an 1850s pioneer girl. Anyone could see she wasn't outfitted like a modern girl.

"You're right," he replied. "We came from New York and New Jersey."

"No!" she almost screamed. "She doesn't belong! Get away!"

Garth stepped backward because he wanted to get Lydia far from the crazy lady. She yelled loud enough to attract attention, and he knew from his time with Sam that usually led to trouble from the authorities.

"Come on, Lydia. We have to find that kiosk before this mall closes again. By the looks of it, that's almost a certainty." He pulled her away, but they had to listen to the woman scream about things in the wall and people who didn't belong for the next couple of minutes. Her ramblings could barely be heard when they made it far down the mall, but the peace was shattered when another woman came out of a boutique in a hurry.

He was certain Lydia was about to get another earful as the soccer mom cupped her hands to shout, but it wasn't directed at anyone in particular. She belted out to the entire mall, "They nuked Las Vegas!"

Garth stopped in his tracks, as did everyone else. For a few moments they all watched the woman run for the exit, but the nervous energy built up as he waited. He shared worried glances with a dozen other shoppers.

Everyone seemed to consider what to do next.

He already knew.

FOUR

***Search for Nuclear, Astrophysical, and Krono-
metric Extremes (SNAKE). Red Mesa, Colorado***

Bob leaned against Faith as they walked through the
halls of SNAKE. After being struck in the face and having
his nose broken, the soldiers had made them go back inside.
Once they discovered Faith and Bob were part of the leadership of the facility, they separated them from the rest of
the scientists.

She pleaded with the grim-looking soldiers. "This man
needs medical attention."

"Be quiet," one of the guards said scornfully. "I need
you both to shut up."

"That's not very polite." Bob chuckled before stopping
himself. It must have hurt his nose.

The young guard held up a shiny black rifle and pointed
it at Bob's face. "Shut up, mister. You will not say another
word."

Faith pulled him away from the guard and shushed him
to make it clear what he was expected to do. She checked to
ensure they weren't going to move right away, then

motioned for Bob to sit on the carpet at the edge of the hallway.

He sat without saying anything, although he grunted as if the act of sitting had hurt his nose too.

She whispered. "Are you trying to get us killed? That guard isn't taking any shit from us."

"I told you," he said disappointedly. "These aren't the same type of military people who were here with General Smith. I think they are from those black-hole prisons we hear about in Eastern Europe. If not there, maybe they did time in Hell. Especially the asshole who hit me."

Faith tried not to laugh as she sat down next to him. "I'm sorry I don't have anything to stop the bleeding. Maybe you could use your shirt."

He turned to her with watery eyes. It looked like he was suffering. "Maybe I could use *your* shirt? Mine is expensive."

She shook her head. "An asshole until the end. Well, you should know—"

Her attention was broken by numerous people walking far down the hallway. It appeared as if dozens of her teammates were being directed down the stairwell.

She wanted to ask a guard but didn't want to get a rifle butt in the face.

Faith gestured to Bob. "It looks like they are putting them downstairs in the auditorium again."

He nodded. "It's the only space big enough to hold all of us. Do you think they'll be all right?"

"How should I know?" she replied.

A small group of workers were separated from the line and marched up the hall toward Faith and Bob.

"Uh-oh," she whispered. "It looks like they found all the department heads."

She didn't know what that meant, although she tried not to read too much into it. General Smith had gathered the senior staff when he came in, so this was probably a lot like that.

"On your feet," the nearest guard commanded her and Bob.

Faith wanted to complain and ask again for medical attention, but she didn't want to anger the lead guard. She helped Bob to his feet and steadied him as he tried to force blood to go back down his nose.

"Hello, Doctor Sinclair," Sunetra said when she was close.

"Shut it!" a guard barked. "No talking."

Sun frowned.

Somehow, the guards had gathered all of her senior staffers and department heads. Belatedly, she thought General Smith's staff had left paperwork explaining the hierarchy in SNAKE.

"March that way," the guard said, pointing in the opposite direction of the larger group going down the stairs.

"Where are you taking us?" she asked in a determined voice. "We have rights."

"You have the right to shut up, miss. If you waive that right, then I have the right to shoot you in the face." He waved his gun in a menacing fashion.

"I'm the director of this facility. You can't talk—"

The guard aimed the scary-looking rifle at her nose. When she looked down the length of the barrel, she found empty blue eyes held no sympathy for her. Slowly, she raised her arms in surrender.

"That way," the guard insisted again.

As they walked down the long corridor toward the front of SNAKE, three more guards joined the procession. Each of them wore the same gray-and-tan camo that reminded her of computer-generated boxes, and they all carried the same black rifles. All of them were young, like they hadn't been in the service long, but none of them looked like they didn't belong. To Faith, they had that same determination shown by General Smith.

"In here," one of the guards said when they reached a seldom-used conference room.

The lights were off, so she couldn't see what was in there. However, when she reached for the light switch, the guard brushed her aside.

"The lights stay off," he cautioned.

It was pitch-black inside, but some light came in from the hallway, letting her make out chairs lined up in rows.

"Sit your asses down. We'll take care of you in a few minutes."

Faith guided Bob to one of the chairs in the middle of the rows.

"Sit," she whispered.

"Is it as dark as it seems, or is my vision going to shit with all this swelling?"

"It isn't your eyes. They have us in conference room number five."

She had trouble figuring out who else filed into the room after her, but she got the sense it was her entire leadership team. No one was allowed to speak, and her focus was on Bob for the moment, so she lost track of numbers.

When the door closed, it left them all in absolute darkness.

"It was nice knowing you," a man said dryly from behind Faith.

"This isn't a murder scene," a woman replied.

"Everyone, this is Faith. I'm sure there's an explanation

for all this. Please remain calm." She closed her eyes, expecting a hidden guard to whack her for talking.

The man behind her continued, "Faith? Your boy Bob is probably out there now giving them the keys to the kingdom. Telling them what he did to fuck us all over with his side project. Now he's going to get us all killed for messing it up."

"I know for a fact that's not true," Faith replied.

"How can you possibly know that?" the man in the darkness replied. She recognized him as part of the computer team. That made him one of Bob's employees.

"Because of this guy." She tapped Bob on the shoulder.

Ten seconds went by, and Bob still hadn't replied.

After another ten, she realized she might have been wrong after all.

Australia, 2am

Zandre's truck skidded up to the front of Destiny's flat.

"Come on! Get in!" he shouted.

She ran and hopped in the passenger-side door. "I'm so glad you made it, Z."

He put the truck into gear and sped out of the parking lot. "You should have gone without me. I'll never forgive myself if you gave up your chance to go to America to wait for me."

Animals squealed in the back compartment of the large truck as they took turns at high speed.

"You brought them?" Her original plan was for Zandre and her to make the case that they needed the boat to sail some of the animal specimens to anxious zoos in North America, but that plan turned out to be overkill. The management of the Sydney Harbor Foundation had decided to go to America anyway, without the animals, once they learned about SNAKE.

"I know you said we wouldn't need them, but I wanted to have them as insurance. By the time we get to the boat, we might need some bargaining power to get aboard."

She scoffed. "The boat was my idea. They'll let me on."

He was unimpressed. "Just like they left you in the forest fire? Dez, these are not the good people you thought they were. This is life and death now, and they'll do anything—*anything*—to keep themselves alive. You should remember that and do the same. Your first act should have been leaving me behind, although I'm glad you didn't."

He steered the truck onto the roadway. Because it was two in the morning, there weren't many cars out, which was part of how he had made it from Canberra to Sydney in record time.

"All we have to do is make it to the *Majestic*," she said slowly, as if she were thinking about the gravity of each word. "If we don't make it, then so be it. I couldn't have spent the rest of my life knowing I left you behind when I could have waited and brought you with me."

She had other friends she could have called. Lots of old boyfriends. A few close girlfriends.

However, despite his enthusiasm for culling the herd, Zandre was a fellow animal-lover. That earned him a special place in her heart.

She'd spent some time over the last few hours texting people she knew, trying to get them to go to America, but none of them believed her. Not one.

Zandre, however, had dropped everything and driven like hell to be with her. She told herself it was because he wanted to save the animals, too, but deep down, she wondered about his real motive.

She leaned to her left as Zandre took another corner. Some animals roared in the back.

"What did you bring?" She pointed to the enclosure on the back of the small box truck.

"Two Tasmanian Tigers and one Duck of Doom. I also brought the body of another animal—something I've never seen before. I figured the boat people would be impressed."

"Let's hope so," she said dryly.

The road ahead would take them along the coast of the inner harbor, but the lighted highway ended abruptly half a kilometer ahead.

"What the fuck?" she said while looking at the blackness.

The ambient light of the city provided enough illumination to see the beach wrap around the harbor. The houses and roadways along the shore were gone, however. The city just stopped, like someone had taken scissors and sliced it away. It was the same thing that happened on the other side of the harbor, where the Sydney Opera House had once stood.

Was the *Majestic* still out there?

Zandre stopped the truck at the edge of the highway.

"What do we do?" he asked.

"Drive that way. We have fuck-all chance if we turn around. The boat has to be at the end of that beach." She pointed into the darkness.

He put it into gear but turned to her for a second. "Thanks for waiting for me. I won't forget this."

"Thanks for always being there for me over the years. I could always count on you, just like my dad said." Zandre wasn't as old as her late father, but he was close. Her dad was a big reason she got into the business of saving animals, and Zandre was the family friend who helped her get

35

started after her father passed. Saving his life was the least she could do to pay him back.

"No worries, mate. Right now, buckle up. We're going off-road."

She hated being the passenger, but Zandre had lived his whole life out in the bush. There was no one better suited to get them across this mini-wilderness right now.

In the back, the Duck of Doom squawked one loud call.

It was almost like it sensed the danger ahead.

Nebraska

The aircraft carrier slumped on the muddy field next to the highway like a beached whale. It leaned to the right, so most of the landing deck was visible. It also had two nasty holes on the right side near the front.

Buck and Connie walked over to a small group of travelers who had gathered next to the highway. Mac stretched the leash as far as it would go, seeming anxious to see and smell new humans.

"What are they doing?" Connie whispered.

"I think they're praying," he replied.

Buck was right. As they walked up, one of the men wrapped up a prayer and said Amen. The others repeated the word.

The group broke up, but Buck caught one of the men.

"Hey, what's happening here?"

The guy stopped, seemingly happy to talk. "A miracle! This ship appeared out of nowhere a few minutes ago, along with a lot of sea water. God is sending us a sign."

"A sign for what?" Connie asked in a friendly way.

"I don't know Bible verses like those folks do, but that man quoted scripture, saying that when the Book of Revelation is upon us, we will be rejoined with our loved ones. This ship came back as part of that. Soon, people will return. We'll all live happily ever after..."

The older gentleman rubbed his gray stubble while looking at the ship. "I sure as hell can't wait. This is the USS *Wasp*, which sunk in World War II. My dad was also killed in that war. It means he's soon to come back!"

Buck tried not to frown. There was nothing about a rusty aircraft carrier sitting in a Nebraska pasture that screamed, "Relatives are coming back from the dead!"

But then he looked at Connie, suddenly reminded of her origin.

She had come back.

FIVE

Sidney, NE

Buck and Connie walked fifty yards toward the USS *Wasp*. Mac ran free. They both decided there was little danger for the excitable pup, and they stuck to a small rise in the muddy field to stay out of the worst of the quagmire.

He thought about the old man's words the whole way. His silence made Connie notice he wasn't cutting jokes or opening his yap at all. Even his interactions with Mac were half-hearted.

"Care to share?" she said, nudging him.

"What were you doing before you came to my time?" he asked nonchalantly.

That made her stop. A cool breeze blew against his back as he halted, too. It was as if the giant ship was colder than the rest of the field.

"Why do you ask?" she inquired skeptically.

"No reason," he said in a not-very-convincing way.

She stuck her hands on her hips just above the fancy belt holding up her jeans.

"Fine," he said with exasperation, before laughing

briefly. "You've got mad interrogation skills. You sure you weren't in the service? FBI, maybe?"

"No delaying," she said in a friendly but determined way.

Buck pointed his thumb over his shoulder at the road. "That guy said he was waiting for his relatives to show up, like this was some kind of Bible story. I was going to write it off as the ravings of a lunatic, except then I thought you might have died back in your time and then came here."

He rubbed his neck. "So, were you in any danger back then?"

She shook her head. "I'm not dead, Buck. I told you when we met. I was coming back from a writer's conference. I stayed in that dumpy motel overnight in 2003. When I woke up, I heard you and the manager arguing in 2020."

"Thank God," he said, relieved.

"I can't believe you'd listen to some random guy you met in a field." She took a step closer. "Besides, if I were dead, I'd be in Yellowstone or hiking in Grand Canyon. I wouldn't be in some shitty field in Nebraska with a World War II battleship—"

"Carrier," he corrected.

She took another step.

"Carrier. Whatever. Listen, the only thing you have to worry about is getting to your son. Stuff like this," she pointed to the *Wasp*, "only serves as distractions. The Bible folks don't have all the answers. Nor do the scientists. Nor does anyone. All we can count on is each other to get us through this."

She was close enough to put her arms around Buck's neck.

"So, now I have a question for you," she said, smiling up at him.

"Shoot." He grabbed her waist out of instinct.

"Are you ever going to kiss me? We've spent two nights together, and I tempted you with that shower towel. We snuggled in the cold last night—"

"It's a hundred degrees outside," he shot back.

"It's ten in your sleeper," she retorted playfully.

He was going to argue some more, but she put a finger over his lips for a moment. "I didn't come here to be a distraction, Buck. As I said, we have to find your son."

He chuckled and pulled her up against his body. "Oh, you've been a huge distraction. I'm usually a man of action, but this time I've been torn by a little voice in my head saying you are going to disappear the second I make a move. You know what I mean? I don't want that to happen."

"So, if we kissed, this ship, the weird weather, and rogue biker gangs would go away?"

Buck gazed at her smiling face. "Of course, I could stand to lose that crap, but I couldn't handle losing you with them."

Her ocean-blue eyes melted.

They leaned in the last few inches and kissed with fiery passion on the muddy field. Time seemed to bleed away as Buck enjoyed being with the woman who'd been instrumental in helping him stay on track toward Garth. Now that he finally had her to himself, he was going to savor it.

Seconds after they locked lips, Mac became restless and nudged his leg. Buck tried to gently push him away, just for a few more seconds, but Connie seemed to notice the commotion, and they both came up for air.

"The dog. He's, uh..."

She pecked him on the lips. "He needs you."

After an instant of admiring her, he finally looked at Mac. The Golden faced the Peterbilt back on the highway and whined a warning as if he believed Buck had left the iron on.

"Well, shit. There goes the neighborhood."

He and Connie separated just enough they could both look at the interstate.

Cars peeled out from where they'd pulled over. People who lingered near the shoulder to take pictures of the ship now ran for their cars. Some of the vehicles slowing down to park suddenly accelerated away.

"What the fuck is their problem?" Buck turned around to look at the ship, halfway expecting it to be rolling toward him, but it appeared exactly as it did a minute earlier.

"We should go find out," Connie said with sadness. "I'm sure it isn't good."

She pulled him toward the Peterbilt, but he planted his feet.

"What is it?" she probed.

"Before we get back to reality, I just want to say that even if you disappear in five minutes, kissing you was worth the risk of making you vanish back to your own time. We make a great team. Thanks for sticking with me."

She stood on her toes and kissed him briefly on the lips. "That goes double for me. But I should warn you: If I do go back to 2003, I'm going to bide my time and come looking for you in 2020."

"I'll watch for you!" He laughed.

He and Connie walked together.

"Come here, Mac," she called to the Golden. After hopping a big mud puddle, he ran over and allowed her to secure the leash again.

"I think he listens to you better than he does me," he said, pointing at the little rascal.

"Of course, he does. He knows you're with me."

"You mean he knows you're with *me*," he joked.

"Oh, that's how it's gonna be?" She pretended to be hurt.

They walked quickly back to the roadway. Most of the spectators were already in their cars, but a few people, including his friends in the convoy, stood in a small group.

When they got close, Eve ran over to them.

"Guys! Big news. There have been nuclear explosions in Nevada and New Mexico!"

"Where in New Mexico?" Connie asked immediately. That was where she was from.

The young recruiter looked flustered. "That's all I know. It literally happened a few minutes ago. That's why everyone took off."

He and Connie joined hands.

"There could be more," he said dryly.

They all ran for their trucks.

Louisville, KY

Garth hurriedly walked Lydia where he wanted to go.

"Come on. We have to keep moving," he said under his breath so as not to scare the other shoppers. Lots of people had heard the woman scream, but he figured if he walked calmly away from where she had yelled the news, the rest of the mall would be unaware.

"They bombed Las Vegas!" a man shouted as he ran deeper into the mall. Numerous people came out of stores after the guy went by.

"Dammit," Garth said quietly. It appeared he was the only person who didn't want to spread the panic.

"What is going on?" Lydia asked. "Why is everyone frightened? Even you?"

That made him take a deep breath. "I'm not scared. It's that I'm trying to think of what I should be doing before I do it. Dad would want me to keep my head, even when everyone else is losing theirs. It's kind of his thing."

"So there *is* reason to be scared?"

"I don't know," he replied. "If the woman was right and there was a nuclear bomb, it would be a million times worse than a little radiation falling from the sky. On the other hand, from what I learned at school and from my dad, there isn't much you can do to prepare for a bomb if it's going to hit you."

He and Lydia trotted through the mall, on the lookout for the familiar logo of his cell phone company. However, running with her made him realize he wasn't ready to burn up in a nuclear inferno. Not just because he didn't want to die, either. He liked hanging out with her.

"Shouldn't we leave?" she asked.

That would be the sensible play—get in the taxi and get as far away from Louisville as possible. Yet, he didn't want to run when he was so close to getting his dad's number. If there was something big coming down on the cities, he might never have another chance to contact him.

"We will. We just have to find—" He saw the distinctive orange banner in a small annex near a side door. "There!"

He grabbed her hand and pulled her toward it at a fast jog.

"It's here!" he said excitedly as he neared the kiosk.

Two scruffy-looking young men trotted by, carrying a long flat-panel television box between them. They watched him intently as if they were worried he was going to try to stop them, but his only response was to use his arm to hold back Lydia so she didn't run into them.

One of the guys nodded what might have been a thank you, and he repeated it back to him. They might have been stealing, but at least they were polite about it.

A distant pop sound reminded him of gunfire.

"This is what I've been looking for." A table and chair stood alone in the middle of the walkway. It was designed to force visitors to see the logo of the cell phone company and encourage them to sign up. An ancient personal computer system sat below the table, hidden from view by the vinyl banner tied between two legs. "But there is no one here."

Lydia searched all around. "How is this table going to help you contact your dad? There isn't even one of your telephones here."

"It will take me too long to explain."

A woman's shriek from several stores down made him wince in sympathy. Whatever was happening out there, he had to hurry.

"So, what are you going to do?"

He bent down and hit the power button for the computer.

"I'm going to pretend I work here."

"What good will that do?" she said, sounding exasperated. "Garth, we should leave."

"I know, and we will. I only need two minutes."

He took a seat and watched the screen load. The boot-up routine for the Windows computer had never seemed longer.

A woman walked by dragging a young boy behind her. He was ten or eleven, the best Garth could guess. The kid kicked and bucked against her firm grip, but he was also crying like a baby. The mother-figure didn't look back at him as she pulled him out the doors.

A male voice spoke through the speakers on the ceiling. "Attention, shoppers. The Saint Matthews Mall will be closing immediately. Please exit safely. Good luck, and God speed to you."

The lights flashed on and off several times, another sign the place was closing.

"Come on!" He half-kicked the computer.

It finally booted to the login screen, but Garth realized he was about to be defeated.

"Shit! I can't get in."

Lydia peered at the computer screen, then looked behind it. "Where is the light coming from?"

He didn't have time for her wonderment, even though he would love to show her everything he could on the internet. It wouldn't be a surprise if he could find pictures of the Oregon Trail. She might recognize the sights.

"These tables are run by kids. I'm sure they wouldn't remember their passwords. It has to be written down somewhere."

He searched around for a few seconds, but there wasn't anything on the table besides the screen, keyboard, or mouse. He lifted the keyboard and mouse, hoping to see the password scrawled on the plastic, but that was a bust.

Garth checked under the monitor but came up just as empty.

He looked under the mouse and keyboard a second time, giving them a closer scrutiny. He was certain he was right.

"Garth, there is a police person coming this way."

He looked up for two seconds. The security guard had come back, evidently without the guys he'd been chasing.

He now ushered shoppers toward the exit. The gates on the stores dropped closed behind him. This time, he had backup. Two armed police officers escorted the guard as he paced down the concourse.

"Come on!" he demanded of the computer.

The keyboard had a small battery compartment on the underside. He snapped it off and saw two gold-colored batteries inside.

"Dammit again!"

He'd come up empty.

The guard and his friends were close. Garth was almost certain he'd been spotted.

"What's that say?" Lydia pointed to the lid for the battery slot. The long piece of plastic had fallen to the table, but a piece of paper had been taped to the back side.

"Lydia, I love you!" He picked up the paper. "The password is Mobileooooooo1."

He righted the keyboard, then typed it in.

The guard peeled off from the police and came toward the table. He was twenty feet away when he said, "Hey, kids. Time to move along. That computer isn't for shoppers. Get out of here. Get home."

"I'm in," he said to himself.

He had no idea where to go inside the computer system once he was there. Most of his computer experience involved loading games he wanted to play. Programming and operating business programs wasn't his thing.

Garth looked at Lydia over his shoulder.

No help there.

He laughed at the futility and started clicking.

SIX

Search for Nuclear, Astrophysical, and Krono-metric Extremes (SNAKE). Red Mesa, Colorado

"Bob, tell them it isn't true. We aren't going to be killed for knowing what happened here."

The guy in the back seemed surprised. "Oh, he's here? Shit."

"Yes, he's here. He was trying to get away, and he got his nose broken for his troubles. I highly doubt he planned that."

"Yeah," Bob finally replied, "I have nothing to do with any of these people. It seems like the military finally made it here in force. A little too much force, if you want my opinion."

Faith felt better, knowing Bob's place. If he betrayed her again, things were going to get nasty between them. As it was, he was almost bearable. She found that to be much preferable to their usual antagonism.

"Faith, where are you?"

"Donald? Oh, no. They brought you here, too?" She

patted Bob on the arm. "I'll be right back. I just want to check on him, okay?"

"Yeah, no problem. I'll be fine." His strained voice suggested the opposite, but she had to know if Donald was all right.

"Talk to me, Donald. I'm coming over."

She tripped her way through the people in other chairs until she heard Dr. Perkins' voice next to her face. She reached out to find his hands searching for her.

"Got ya!" she said.

"What are we doing in here?" he asked.

She didn't have any clue, but didn't want to build up the fiction that they were going to be offed. "I think they brought in the upper echelons of the project to keep us safe from the terrorists."

A couple of people scoffed, but she ignored them.

She continued. "Are you in your wheelchair? How are you?"

"I'm in the chair, yes. As for how I am..." He paused for ten or fifteen seconds. "Faith, I'm not doing well." He coughed for emphasis, and she noticed his breathing was wheezy and wet. "My heart is weak."

Faith squeezed his hands for a moment, then got up. "I'm going to get you some help."

"I don't think—"

She interrupted. "Don't bother. I'm doing it."

Faith felt her way to the wall, then to the front door. The whole reason for shoving them into the room was a mystery to her, but instead of making her curious as to the why, she became angry that it had happened at all. Whoever was in charge, they had to know they were putting Donald in extreme danger.

She banged on the wooden door with both fists.

"We need medical assistance in here!"

Her shouting seemed to agitate the other people in the room. A few of them admonished her.

One of the women hissed, "Don't antagonize them."

Her reaction was unexpected. "I'll do whatever I damn well please. I'm in charge of this facility, and we're fucking doing this my way, not yours."

She waited for a second to see if the argument would continue, but the woman backed down.

"Now," she said, banging her fists again. "Let us out of here!"

A person on the outside jiggled the handle.

"Stand back. We're opening the door."

Faith did as instructed. "I'm away."

The guard opened the door a crack. The light from the windows across the hallway forced her to block the sun with her hand. Even in the few minutes she'd been in the dark, her eyes had become accustomed.

A pair of figures was shoved through the door. The first was a woman from her physics team, and the second was her assistant.

"Missy!" she said as she caught her friend in her arms.

The door slammed shut again.

"I've got you," she said to Missy. "You are both fine. Please find a chair and sit down."

Faith guided her friend to an empty chair. "I'm so glad to see you again."

Missy held her hand, as if unwilling to let her boss out of her reach. "I missed you, too. I can't believe this is happening."

"Why are you here?" In her brief look at the people inside the room, most were senior-level staff. Missy was an administrative assistant, not a scientist.

"Well, since General Smith and his people arrived, I've been doing work for them. They saw me in the auditorium that first night, and they put me in charge of food and drink for the staff being kept here against their will. I kept meaning to come up and visit you, especially after I heard there was a bombing attempt on your life, but I couldn't get away."

Faith took a stab at what had changed. "But now they have more people to help you."

"I don't know. They are moving everyone around. I was kind of in the lead down in the auditorium, so I guess they assumed I was important. That has to be why they brought me upstairs to you guys."

"Yeah, everyone in the leadership team from both groups is here. Dr. Perkins was brought in too."

"Oh," Missy said sadly. "How is he?"

"Okay, for now," Faith answered.

"Hi, Donald," Missy called into the darkness.

"Hello, Ms. Paulus. I hope you are doing well."

"I am. We've been—"

A blue dot appeared on the interactive whiteboard at the end of the room.

"Something's happening," Faith said in a loud voice.

The digital whiteboard was basically a video screen as big as the wall. A presenter could draw on the board or interact with it on their computer screen.

The dot became a video, which finally provided some light to the room. Two dozen people sat in rows of chairs facing the screen.

Faith squeezed Missy's hand. "I've got to get to my seat. We'll talk after this is over. Good to see—well, hear—you."

Missy laughed. "I can't wait."

An introductory screen flashed on the wall as Faith made her way to the seat next to Bob.

'TOP SECRET Codeword.'

After a brief fade-to-black, another panel displayed on the wall, and the audio started.

"Ladies and gentlemen," the voice said, "Azurasia Heavy Industries, in conjunction with the United States Government Procurement Division, proudly presents the Four Arrows Project..."

Red Mesa, CO

Phil made a split-second decision to remain hidden rather than engage the group of men approaching. Even if they were Soviet shock troops, attacking at one-versus-four odds was a bad play. The element of surprise wouldn't necessarily ensure victory, either. Plus, he had three unarmed charges behind him.

"Keep trying the radio, Grafton," one of the approaching men said in a quiet voice.

Grafton?

The men closed the distance as they walked through the woods. Once they were within twenty yards, he knew who they were.

He crouched a bit lower to ensure he wasn't in their line of sight, then called, "Land of Enchantment."

The approaching soldiers dove for cover, as he'd expected.

Ten seconds later, a man replied, "Land of Lincoln."

It was a valid response to his challenge. He and Ethan had set it up for the team in case they were separated. They were the mottos for each of their home states.

Phil held his position without looking around his tree. "Colonel Knight?"

"Colonel Stanwick?" came the reply.

"I have three men with me. We're coming out."

Ethan and his men came out at the same time.

"Holy shit, Phil, am I glad to see you!" He and Phil shook hands before he continued, "We've been wandering around these woods for hours. The radio is dead. My phone is dead." Ethan leaned in close, so only Phil would hear him. "I don't even think we're in Switzerland."

Phil pointed to Sanchez. "Tell Lieutenant Colonel Knight where we are."

"Colorado, sir. This is Red Mesa, and you are on top of the SNAKE supercollider."

Ethan turned serious, like he'd struck pay dirt on intel. "You're Air Force. Were you guarding this place?"

"Yes, sir. I'm with the NORAD contingent from Peterson. However, Colonel Stanwick had us stake out the exits because a new unit has moved in. We saw them assault one of the scientists."

Phil was satisfied with the report of his subordinate, but he added his own thoughts. "Sir, it was only one incident, but Private Sanchez was right in his initial observations. It wasn't the behavior I'd expect from a professional US Army soldier."

Ethan leaned against a tree and brushed some pine needles out of his hair. "I'm still trying to wrap my head around why we aren't in Switzerland. Any theories?" He looked at Phil.

"Ever see *Star Trek*? I think we were beamed from one side of the planet to the other. Not sure how, but the city of Denver is visible a few hundred yards down this path, although I wouldn't check it out now that the sun is up. They have guards on all the exits."

"So, let me get this straight," Ethan said as he stood up. "We're now in Colorado at the facility we were trying to help by shutting down CERN, and a rogue military unit has taken it over?"

Phil nodded. "It sounds nuts even to me. The only way to be sure is to approach one of their guard posts and see if we can get a handle on who they are."

It was sound military doctrine, and again, it all came back to the strangeness of the situation. If the world were perfectly normal, they'd walk right up to the other soldiers and shoot the shit rather than bullets. However, after beaming across the world, it was prudent to treat everyone as an enemy until the truth could be established.

Ethan nodded. "So, let's go meet the neighbors."

Nebraska

Buck's euphoria from kissing Connie faded fast. As they ran back to the Peterbilt and got the convoy back on the highway, he returned to worrying about Garth.

"They said the nukes hit in Nevada and New Mexico. You are from New Mexico. Did they say where they hit?" He pressed the dial of the radio, searching for answers.

"I hope it wasn't Santa Fe. God help them if it was. I know a lot of good people from there."

Buck found a news channel, but they were talking about SNAKE again.

"Dammit, I want to hear about those nukes. Are we at war?" Ever since the President had announced the United States wouldn't drop bombs on enemy powers, he'd worried that was exactly what would happen. The generals wouldn't be able to resist using their weapons one last time.

"Garth isn't picking up, Buck. And my son's phone number, of course, still rings forever."

"Keep trying," he said distractedly. The two lanes of the highway ahead were filled with cars and trucks, as if the pair of lanes condensed down to one. "We've got construction or a wreck up ahead."

The CB chirped.

"What now?" he asked with exasperation.

"This is Sparky. Buck, we need to talk when we stop again. I'm beginning to think our goal of making it across the country might be slipping away."

Not a chance.

Monsignor popped on. "If that ship had landed a few yards to the south, it would have blocked the entire highway. Who knows what we're going to find as we continue? We should at least plan for a contingency."

"Damn, he's right," Buck said to Connie with frustration. "I've known for a while that we aren't going to make it to the East Coast. Monsignor might make it to his terminal in Illinois, but Eve probably isn't going to get all the way to Massachusetts to deliver those televisions. A shame, too, since there is probably a big demand for people who want to see the Apocalypse on a big screen tv."

He chuckled at his joke, but Connie didn't crack a smile. She held up his phone. "Still nothing. I'll try again in a few minutes."

Buck looked over his shoulder at Big Mac. "Hey, you, come here a minute."

The Golden hopped off the sleeper bed and came up next to his seat. Buck took a few seconds to scratch behind the dog's ears because he found it relaxing. Mac apparently did, too.

When he was ready, he picked up the CB. "This is Buck. I know I gave you all a pep talk about not dropping your loads and going home, but things have changed. We've seen some wild shit the last couple of days, but that ship on dry land was the kicker. I think Sparky has it figured out. We aren't going to make it too much farther to the east."

He let off the mic and looked at Connie for strength. The next words out of his mouth were going to sound like a surrender, but he knew it wasn't that at all. His mission was different from theirs.

"But I'm still going that way, at least for a little while. My son is heading toward us on Interstate 64, so I'm going to drop south and jump on that highway until I find him. Then..." he took a deep breath. "I'm going to come back west and go to Denver."

Buck set down the mic to wait for the reaction. He expected three different voices complaining to him about going back on his promise to take them to their destinations, but the channel remained silent.

After ten seconds, he picked it up again. "Did you all catch that? Over."

"Yeah, Buck, we heard you," Sparky replied. "It's as good a plan as any."

Eve spoke next, as if Sparky had handed her the microphone. "The electronics in my trailer won't rot, so if I take a detour to find safety in Denver for a little while, no one will starve. Except maybe me, if I don't get paid." She and Sparky laughed on the airwaves. "My parents are in Seattle, but I'm not ready to turn tail and run back to them. I've got plenty of fuel right now, so Sparky and I will hang with you while we make sure you find your son. Then we can all turn around and head for the Mile-High City."

"Shit, guys. That means a lot. What are your thoughts, Monsignor?" Buck inquired.

"Yeah, I'll have to think about it. I only have to get to the Mississippi River near St. Louis, so I can follow you down to the 64. I'll decide whether to turn around once we find your son. I hope you do, Buck."

"Thanks, guys. I don't know how I got lucky enough to run into you three."

Once he was done on the CB, he didn't waste a second.

"Can you try my son again?"

SEVEN

Louisville, KY

As the security guard neared, Garth tried to think what his best friend Sam would do.

"I work here. Just closing up for my boss."

When the guard didn't immediately laugh at him, he pressed his luck.

"I don't get paid enough to work with all these crazies, though." He pointed down the mall, where numerous people still ran back and forth with treasures they had stolen from the stores.

The guard lazily dragged his hand over the table as he walked by. "You have five minutes. Everyone is supposed to be out of here. The mall owner wants it all locked down before the looting gets any worse."

Garth went back to the keyboard, happy for the grace period.

"I have to find where they keep the numbers..."

Lydia stood close, looking over his shoulder.

He clicked around the menu for a few seconds, but then

realized he needed to think like an employee. They wouldn't bury the application in a menu. It would be—

"Got it!" The company's logo was on the desktop, and after clicking it, he was taken into the master application.

"Holy shiz," he said, as if he'd just opened a treasure chest. "We've got it all."

The security guard shouted from about ten stores down the concourse. "Stop him!"

One of the police officers wielded a black baton, which he swung into the ribs of a man running out of an athletic shoe store. Garth heard the crack of bone from a hundred feet away.

"Must hurry," he said quietly.

After clicking in and out of screens designed for data entry, he finally found one with a search bar on it.

"Search by phone number, customer number, or plan start date. Why can't I search by name?" He was anxious because the rest of the mall seemed to resist the message of closing time being announced by the security team.

Down the way, several men darted out of the shoe store loaded with boxes. There were too many for the police to catch, although they tried to bash kneecaps of anyone they could. Most of the runners went away from Garth's little table, but one of them got around the guards and ran his way.

He brushed sweat off his brow as he hit more dead ends inside the program. "Geez. This is worse than a final back in school."

A few seconds went by, then the runner passed his table. He saw the guy dash out the side door in his peripheral vision.

"Think, man." He clicked some more screens, always looking for the search bar.

"He stole the cash!" a woman screamed to the police.

Garth didn't look up. Whatever else happened, he needed that phone number.

Lydia stood up against him and put her hand on his shoulder, but he didn't think it had anything to do with romance.

"Those people are hurting each other," she said distantly.

He found a screen marked 'Lost and Misplaced' and decided to check it out.

"Jackpot!" It had a button for search, but it included the option to look up by customer name.

He typed in his dad's info and waited for the result. A small hourglass began twirling in the middle of the screen. Ten seconds went by before another distraction made him glance up to ensure he wasn't in danger.

A second bad guy hustled by at a full sprint. To Garth, it was like watching a television show about cops, because the guy protected one bright blue shoe box under each arm. Behind him, the security guard was in hot pursuit.

A small chime echoed from the speakers of the computer.

"I've got it!" His dad's name and address showed on the screen, but more importantly, his cell number was listed below it. All he had to do was...

"Shit. You don't have a pencil, do you? I need something to write this down." He looked at Lydia like he'd just asked for a laser pistol. There was no way the pioneer girl would have one on her.

"My quill is back in the wagon," she said desperately. "I'm sorry."

The guard ran by as he chased the shoe thief, but he

also noticed the two of them still at the computer. "Get the fuck out of here!"

"My word," Lydia replied. "What is happening?"

"Dad would say this place is losing its shit. We have to get this over with. Can you remember three numbers?"

Garth looked at his dad's phone number and read the first three over and over, hoping she would memorize them. He didn't have to worry about the area code because it was the same as his.

"She's got a gun!" a man hollered.

He angled his head so he could see around the computer monitor. Beyond the struggling officers and the shoe store, a lone woman stood in the middle of the mall with a silver gun in her hand. She didn't point it at anyone, but kept it close to her chest as if she wasn't sure what to do with it.

"It's our friend," Garth exclaimed. "What is she doing?"

It was the insane woman he had bumped into earlier.

"Some of you shouldn't be here!" She shouted the words several times as both officers oriented on her. One of the looters they'd detained got off the floor and ran for it. At the last second, he picked up one of the blue shoe boxes to complete the theft.

Despite the distance, the woman pointed at Garth and Lydia. "That girl doesn't belong. I told you all! I see them!" She let out loud sobs.

"It's like Dad said; people are losing their shit."

Garth got back to the screen. "I have to remember my part." He stared at the last four digits of his dad's phone number with the hot intensity of a dying sun. His life literally depended on committing them to memory.

The woman with the gun sounded desperate. "I'm like

them. I don't belong. I shouldn't be here." She sniffled a few times, then howled.

Garth looked up to see what she was going to do next.

She extended her arm so the toy gun was pointed at the cops.

"I'm going to kill you all!"

He almost laughed at how stupid she was acting, because she couldn't hurt anyone with a toy gun. And he was certain that was what it was because he'd picked it up off the floor for her.

"It's a fake," he said to himself. Then, realizing what she was doing with it, he jumped out of his chair. Garth intended to shout a warning to the police, but he didn't get the chance.

Gunshots exploded as both police officers put multiple rounds into the troubled woman. Lydia covered her ears as the dull concussions rumbled past them.

Much too late to make a difference, he yelled to the cops, "It's a toy gun!"

The runner tossed his blue shoebox on the floor as he ran by Garth's table, probably thinking the shots were meant for him. The guy never looked back, and almost crashed through the glass-paned exit door as he escaped to the outside.

"We should go," he said hesitantly as he looked around. "That way." He pointed in the direction of the nearest set of doors.

Before he left, he got one last look at the wild scene playing out down the mall. The lady with the silver gun was crumpled in a heap in the middle of the floor. One of the police officers prodded her a little as if to see if she had any life in her. He also kicked the gun away from the corpse, although it skidded and hopped on the tile in a weird way—almost like it didn't weigh anything.

That confirmed it was the toy gun.

One of the officers peered back at him. Garth couldn't read his expression, but he felt bad for the guy. He and his buddy had been forced to shoot an unarmed woman because she was acting nuts.

As he ran out the door with Lydia, he wondered if the dead woman had known what she was doing when she raised the fake gun in front of the police, or if she was as insane as she sounded. And how did the woman know Lydia didn't belong? Was it the obvious pioneer clothing, or did she have some skill that allowed her to identify time-traveling people? He remembered the woman pointing to others in the mall, too. How many were there?

So many questions.

To put it all out of his mind, he recited the four numbers.

He understood those.

I-80, Nebraska

The slowdown on the interstate was caused by a white passenger van. It was parked in the right-hand lane, but there were no people around it. Both of the eastbound lanes merged into one line until traffic passed the van.

"They might have run out of gas," he said to Connie as they rolled by.

She let out a taut laugh. "Could have at least pulled off the roadway."

"I could push them off, kind of like I did with your car." He smiled at her, always aware he owed her big-time for destroying her Volkswagen Beetle. Even if it had some criminal bikers inside, he was the one who had rammed it.

"We ain't got time for that, darlin'," she drawled.

He checked the side mirror next to her. The van was already a hundred yards behind them. "No, I guess we don't."

Minutes later, they were back to their comfortable routine of roving across the FM and AM radio dials as well as dialing Buck's phone. Connie had just grabbed it off the charger when it rang in her hand.

It startled her so much she dropped it on Mac, who was keeping watch under her legs.

"Sorry, boy!" She hurriedly picked it back up and looked at the caller ID.

"It's Garth!"

"That's my boy!" Buck burst out. He held out his hand and took the phone. His heart pounded in his throat as if failing to connect with this one call would be the end of the world. He took a deep breath, then clicked the green button to answer.

"Garth! Thank God!"

A short pause greeted him. Then, a man's deep voice replied, "Who is this?"

Buck held the phone away from him so he was able to read the caller ID. It showed Garth's smiling face, along with his phone number. He put it back to his ear.

"This is Buck. I'm talking to Garth's phone. Where is my son?"

Traffic picked up, but he coasted along just under the speed limit as he tried to listen.

Connie put her hand on his leg, as she always did when it was obvious something was amiss. This time, however, it provided no comfort.

"Hey, boss," the man on the line chattered, "there is someone talking on this black box. He says this belonged to his son."

A dark chuckle came from the other person.

"Look, I don't know who this is, but I need to talk to my son. Is he there?"

A new man came onto the line. "This is Frank Squire. I'm in charge. I ask the questions."

Buck's blood pressure went to fire-hydrant strength in an instant. Every ounce of his Marine Dad brain wanted to cuss out the other man, but he had to be smart if he wanted real answers.

He gritted his teeth. "Sure, Mr. Squire. Fire away."

"Where are you? This black box has a man's picture in this window, but you look far away."

His avatar on Garth's phone showed him standing in the back yard of their home. He couldn't even remember why Garth had taken that photo, but he thought it was from a summer barbeque with Sam's family.

"I'm on the highway in Virginia," he lied, because he wanted to give the impression he wasn't far away. Garth's last known position had him driving toward I-64, so he was likely in that state.

"Virginny, eh?" the man said. He had an odd accent, like he was a mobster from an old movie. "You must really want your son bad. I think I saw him not long ago in a gas station."

"Is he all right?" Buck asked with superhuman restraint.

The man chuckled. Buck clenched his jaw at bear-trap levels of compression because it wasn't a friendly laugh.

"That depends. Does your son have messy hair, wear a funny-looking undershirt, and hang out with a girl who looks like she ate porridge with the Three Little Bears?"

Buck had no idea what his son was wearing, but Garth had described Lydia as someone who had come out of the past. She would likely dress like a primitive.

He drew in a deep breath, sure they knew something.

"Yes, my son is traveling with a young woman who matches that description. Is he okay?"

Just answer the damned question.

"Ah. Yes. It came back to me, you see? Me and Benny knocked over a liquor store yesterday. He and the dame were there, but they were mouthy. We had to make an example out of them. Each of them ate a bullet. Sorry for your loss."

The man laughed in a malicious tone, then the line went dead.

Buck felt like he was going into another blackout tunnel, but this time it wasn't caused by the weird lights in the sky.

Anger swelled inside him like jet fuel being thrown on a campfire.

"What the fuck just happened?" he said in confusion.

"What did they say?" Connie squeezed his leg. "Is Garth..." her voice wavered. "Is he hurt?"

One hand remained on the wheel, but he wasn't looking at the road. He held the phone in front of him like it was going to stab someone.

Buck's confusion fused with his lingering anger. "What the motherfucking hell was that?"

He stomped on the brakes and veered into the break-down lane on the right side of the highway.

The CB lit up, but he wasn't interested.

A red haze shrouded his eyes as if the anger manifested itself in his vision. It made it hard to see the front of his phone while he dialed Garth's number.

"This better be one of his goddam practical jokes," he groused.

The phone rang several times, but the mobster guy's voice greeted him. "I said your son is dead. Don't you get it? I'm tossing this phone. You are about to hear it jump in a lake."

Buck roared into the phone. "Listen, you fucking piece of dog shit, if you fucking harmed my son, I'm going to drive my fucking forty-thousand-pound truck right through your fucking teeth!"

There was no response for ten seconds.

"You finished?" The voice snickered.

"I swear to God!"

"Sorry, friend. I hated to kill a cute kid like that, but it couldn't happen to a shittier father. I don't think you and me would get along at all. Not one bit."

"You are fucking *dead*!" he spat.

"Goodbye," the man said in a businesslike voice. A hissing sound followed after a couple of seconds, like he'd tossed Garth's phone. Some odd noises came through for a moment, then it went dead.

Buck sat there fuming as he fought the logic of what he'd heard. Garth wasn't dead. He couldn't be. And certainly not by some asshole like the cretin he'd been talking to. His boy was smarter than that.

Connie leaned over and spoke with a wobble in her voice. "What happened?"

Buck's internal fire reached the breaking point. He thought one more time about those few words which had ruptured his heart.

"Your son is dead..."

Without thinking, he wound up his arm and threw the phone as hard as he could against the front windshield.

Then he broke down.

EIGHT

***Search for Nuclear, Astrophysical, and Krono-
metric Extremes (SNAKE). Red Mesa, Colorado***

Faith watched with rapt attention as the movie showed scenes of scientists working in a facility a lot like hers.

"The University of Chicago was the control collider—"

"They don't have a supercollider there," a man said from behind Faith.

A woman shushed him, which was good because she would have done the same thing.

"The second collider was located at Malmstrom Air Force Base in Montana. Together, they formed the two endpoints for the Quantum Bridge Project. As required by order of the Director of Operations in the United States Government Weapons Requisition Program, this is the executive summary of the results."

"Holy shit," Faith let slip.

Thankfully, no one shushed *her*.

The screen displayed a line-drawn map with a small circle on each side. On the right, the circle ran under a park and a few blocks inside a city labeled as Chicago. The left half of the map had a similar ring under the runway of an airport labeled as Malmstrom AFB, Montana. Between the two, block letters indicated the map was not drawn to scale.

"The primary hypothesis of this experiment centered around the viability of the purposeful transfer of data on an energy beam linking both supercolliders."

Faith cringed at the scientific gobbledygook her peers were famous for using.

"However, as was discovered by both teams, energy inserted on the Chicago side changed its properties during the transit period."

The film changed from the map to a video shot of what was obviously a laser beam.

"The bridge was supposed to be a quantum link between two high-energy sources, a powered transmitter on one side and a powered receiver on the other. However, despite rigorous attempts at equalizing energy levels at origin and terminus, we were unable to achieve equilibrium."

A split screen appeared. The white-hot laser shot into a black box on the right side of the screen, while a much larger beam came out of a small black metal enclosure on the left side.

"The aperture on the origin side was six centimeters. The focused laser was only six millimeters at insertion, well within design tolerances. On the terminus side, the aperture was six centimeters, one hundred times the size of insertion. So the laser was amplified one hundred times but as we all know, laser output can be increased without a concurrent increase in power, but I don't think that's the case here. I believe there we probably have an exponential increase in output power."

Several people expressed amazement. To Faith, it

appeared as if the laser went in as a tiny pinpoint, but it came out in a beam as thick as a softball.

"How did they do it over all those miles?" a woman asked from somewhere near the front of the room. "This is amazing."

Faith restrained herself from being critical of her team. She was interested in the answer, too. No one was there to answer them, though, and the film continued.

Bob leaned over and whispered. "They are bringing you in as accomplices. I've seen this film. I know how it ends."

"They showed this to you?" Faith whispered back.

"Not this exact thing, but I knew they had a smaller pair of colliders. They needed something to prove the theory before they went big time. They let me study these results so I could ensure there were no gotchas in the Four Arrows Project."

"I guess they weren't too happy with your due diligence, were they?" She made no effort to hide her hip-deep sarcasm.

"I'll be honest with you," he said glumly, "I really thought they were going to kill me when the military stormed in. Both times."

Faith didn't know how she felt about his plight. It served him right, she figured, for doing all this behind her back, but she still thought he was being overly dramatic about the forces driving this.

The film droned on for ten minutes, with scientific formulas and numerous scientists offering their interpretations of the test. She was interested in all of it, but it soon became overwhelming. If she wasn't killed, like Bob feared, she was going to request to see the film again so she could take notes.

Her interest piqued when she recognized one of the

scientists on the screen. It was Doctor Kyle Johnson of MIT, the guy she'd been trying to contact at CERN for the past several days.

"We realized right away that this experiment delivered results with applications far beyond the data transmission and reception it was designed to test. Imagine having the ability to fire a modest laser into a fifty-centimeter aperture on this end and have it come out of a five-hundred-meter ring on the far side. An aircraft carrier would vaporize in an instant. Entire cities could be erased once the technological hurdles for building larger rings are solved. This might have applications in space travel. It might be possible to visit quantum parallels. We simply don't know."

I guess you found out, asshole.

The science was wonderful, but Dr. Johnson and his military masters had left a lot to be desired in how they handled safety. And all for a superweapon? It seemed a terrible waste.

Dr. Johnson continued speaking.

"But all of this paled once we examined the file footage of the exit aperture. Please observe."

The film played the same footage of the laser exiting on the Montana side. The bright laser ended at a heavy piece of black metal, which she assumed was a lead shield. A second camera flickered on, showing the same lab from a different angle.

At first, the laser had her full attention. It was a marvel of technology by itself, because by all indications, it was wrecking the laws of energy and mass since the beam coming out was infinitely brighter and bigger than the one going in.

People around Faith began to gasp and point.

"What the fuck is that?" someone blurted.

"Holy shit," Bob exhaled.

The film played, but Faith was no longer looking at the laser. The second feed showed a scientist standing behind the lead shield. He was the center of everyone's attention.

"What you are seeing is real," the film narrator went on. "There are no edits in this take."

"Oh, come on," she said aloud.

The man was dressed in a white lab coat, exactly like Faith and all her friends wore at SNAKE when they were inside the belly of the beast. However, the man on the screen flickered as the experiment went on. His hair was combed one way one second, and another way a moment later.

He wore glasses for several moments, then they went away. Ten seconds later, the glasses came back with different frames.

Faith stood up and moved down the aisle. She fumbled her way along the side of the room until she was next to the video wall. By the time she made it, the changes to the man were becoming more frequent.

His hair changed several times a second.

The color of his smock morphed from white to gray to any number of bright colors, like a kaleidoscope being rotated at a hundred miles an hour.

Then he shifted into a woman.

Then she was black.

"It's the shift," Faith said to herself. "I'll be damned. This is what we've been doing."

In the film, the laser finally turned off.

The scientist behind the lead plate returned to how he had looked when the experiment started.

The split screen maintained the same views, but the scientists walked around like they were breaking down the equipment. Faith believed Dr. Johnson, or someone like him, was going to come on and explain what just happened, but the narrator jumped on instead.

"And this concludes the executive summary of the Quantum Bridge project. Please direct all questions to your supervisor."

The lights came on.

All eyes were on her.

Red Mesa, CO

Phil volunteered to go up to the guards at one of the exits of the SNAKE lab. They'd made it close to the front of the facility, so several of the concrete bunkers were within walking distance. It was originally how the three airmen planned to get back to their unit, although Phil convinced them to wait.

"Sanchez, you want to go with me? Together we might be able to convince them we belong out here." He handed his rifle to Ethan for safekeeping, but he kept his sidearm.

"Will do, sir."

Ethan went over the plan one last time, then sent them on their way. Phil and Sanchez walked down the wooded pathway rather than zig-zag through the foliage like the rest of the team.

"So, you guys like working in Colorado?" he asked to spark conversation. It wasn't just to be polite to his wing-man; he also wanted the guards to hear them coming from a hundred yards away.

"It's nice for my family. Clean air, and lots of sun. My wife gets a nice tan."

"Sounds like heaven," Phil replied. He didn't have a wife to watch tan, but he could imagine what it would be like. After so many tours overseas, starting a family sounded right on point at that moment.

"Peterson is a nice place, too. I—"

"Halt! By order of the United States military, you are to stop and prepare to be detained!" The guard yelled it with the enthusiasm of a drill sergeant during a shark attack.

"Stay frosty," Phil whispered to Sanchez.

Louder, Phil said, "I'm with the Third Ranger Battalion, 75th Ranger Regiment, US Army. What unit have I found?"

There were two guards, each with M4s. One of them was already on a radio, and the other took a few steps toward Phil, weapon drawn.

He held up his hands. "Easy. We're friendlies."

"Not possible. There are no friendlies out here. You are to stop your fucking walking and wait until I tell you what to do."

Phil managed to get within about twenty feet, which was close enough to see the guard's unit patch, confirm his rank, and ensure he was outfitted in official BDUs. He felt a lot better when he confirmed they weren't dealing with terrorists or mercenaries. A real US Army sergeant would have to follow protocols, just like him.

"We just want to go home," Phil replied in a still-friendly voice. "I'm from New Mexico, in fact. What about you?"

"Fuck, you don't get it, guy? Shut your pie-hole!"

"Well, you didn't say I needed to be quiet. What's going on here?"

Sanchez shifted on his feet, and Phil got the message. His partner was nervous at his bold talk.

Phil, however, needed to keep pressing.

"Is there any way you could get us a lemonade while

we're waiting?" he said in a just-off-the-beach way. "I'm really parched."

The soldier lined up his rifle and fired a three-round burst into the pine needles at their feet.

Fear ricocheted through Phil's middle as if the bullets had entered his body.

That should be enough.

Australia

Zandre and Destiny drove over the sand dunes near the edge of the water as they rushed to get to the *Majestic*. Zandre had apparently been born behind the wheel of his truck, because he seemed to know how to avoid pits and rocks as they cruised through the night.

He went faster than she felt was safe, but all she could do was hold onto the door handle to keep from flopping around in her seat. The truck went up the short dunes, then slammed back down the far sides. Somehow the vehicle held together.

The animals in the back complained about every hit.

Zandre came over a final sand dune, flew about three meters off the ground, and smashed down onto hard pavement again.

People and animals shrieked in shock and pain when the truck's frame struck concrete. It rebounded on its tires and the driver never let off the gas, but he appeared as shaken as she was.

"Damn, Z, where'd you learn to drive?"

He laughed like he'd meant to do that, but he got serious when a grinding noise emerged from the engine compartment.

"We're well and truly fucked, Dez. This thing has had it."

The engine made other noises that sounded like a metal hammer was repeatedly striking an anvil.

"We threw a rod," he barked.

"Are we going to— There! The docks!" She pointed to a well-lit series of boat slips. "You have to make it." Inside, she was singing praises to the heavens that the boat docks were still in existence. The sand dunes had once been a heavily-populated neighborhood near the waterfront and next to the shipping port. Now it was gone.

"We're not stopping now," he replied.

He drove the truck across a parking lot, around some shipping containers, and underneath a giant loading crane. By the time he reached the dock's edge, smoke billowed out from the edges of the hood.

He parked at the base of a large blue and green ship. "The *Majestic*, as promised, mate," Zandre said with celebration in his voice. "Watch your step exiting the vehicle, or you might scratch it."

She glared at him like she couldn't believe he would make a joke at a time like that, but then she hopped out and ran to the back door. Zandre, however, got out and ran toward the walkway to the ship.

"Wait!" she called out. "We need to unload the animals."

"Hold that thought. We want to get ourselves on board first."

She didn't like that idea, since the tigers were making weird sounds in the sealed cages. However, it couldn't hurt to make it known that they had arrived.

"I'll be right back," she said to the animals inside the truck and trotted up the gangway with Zandre.

The ship defied description. It was fifty meters long, with an enclosed bridge about ten meters off the main deck. It was shaped a lot like a fishing trawler, with a streamlined front and a low deck in back filled in with several small cranes. The main hull was painted orange, and prominently featured the kangaroo-with-a-Mohawk logo of the foundation.

The main deck was a disorganized mess of crates, coolers, and cardboard boxes, like a flea market had fallen through a funnel and its contents had dumped everywhere on the ship.

"What the bloody hell happened here?" she asked rhetorically.

"Ahoy!" a man shouted from the middle deck, just below the bridge. "You guys want to chuck that latch on the gangplank? Captain says we're pushing off."

Destiny thought she recognized the young man. He'd been one of the students on the recent expedition, but she couldn't dredge up his name while also worrying about the animals down in the truck.

"We have animals to rescue," she replied in a determined voice. "We can unload them in fifteen minutes!"

Deckhands came out from among the boxes and crates like rats in a garbage dump. They didn't look at Zandre and Dez but instead got busy tossing off the ropes holding them to the pier.

Zandre spoke quietly. "It doesn't look like we'll need the animals after all. What's your play?"

The engines rattled the deck under her feet, and it was obvious the captain wasn't joking around. They'd made it to the ship with only minutes to spare, which was a miracle she wouldn't forget. Yet she was also concerned about those being left behind.

She looked over the side at the smoking truck. There might not be any time to get the animals on board, but it was still possible to jump to the gangplank and go let them out of their cages. Otherwise, they were going to die in there.

She had only a few seconds to decide...

Nebraska

Buck did everything in his power not to shed any tears. It wasn't so much a macho thing, as he didn't want to admit his boy was dead. Despite the obvious fact that he'd been talking to a real asshole on Garth's phone, he couldn't quite believe anyone would shoot a couple of kids for being "mouthy."

He's not dead. No fucking way.

Connie, however, had no such qualms. She'd gotten out of her seat, wrapped herself around Buck, and sobbed for the both of them.

"This is not happening," he said with calm determination. The anger had burned hot when he had thrown his phone, but it had faded fast once he knew Garth's phone had been destroyed. He didn't want to be mad at his two close friends.

"I'm so sorry, Buck. This isn't how it should be."

He put his arm around her back to console her, but also rubbed against Big Mac. The pup always knew when important things were afoot in the cabin, as if he could read minds. He'd come out of his sleeping area under Connie's feet and sat on his haunches between the seats.

"He can't be gone," he replied. "My boy is not fucking dead in this nightmare world." Buck shook off the notion that maybe Garth would come back, like the religious guy said was happening to the time travelers.

"I know," Connie added, with more tears.

"And neither is your son," he said, squeezing her hard.

"I know," she repeated without conviction.

Dammit. Pull yourself together, Marine.

"Fuck!" he screamed to discharge more of his anger and guilt. Gently, he pushed Connie off and over to her seat. "This doesn't change anything. I'm driving east until I see him alive or I see his...belongings. That's all there is to it."

"Are you sure?" she asked with a sniffle.

His mission wasn't going to change simply because some anonymous jagoff had picked up Garth's phone and made an outrageous claim. But the mental wall holding back his emotions was in mortal danger of crumbling down if he sat and wallowed in self-doubt for another second.

Buck started the Peterbilt.

He bit his lips before speaking to Connie. "Let's keep cranking out the miles."

NINE

Louisville, KY

Garth and Lydia ran out of the mall but only found more chaos. Since the police and mall watchman had stressed the urgency of the evacuation, people got into their cars and drove like the hounds of hell nipped at their heels. Screams, tire squeals, and the crunch of fenders were everywhere.

"Where is the tacks-see, Garth?"

Normally, when his dad took him to the mall, he didn't pay attention to anything beyond his mobile phone screen, but since he was in charge of their ride, he had noted the name of the store at the edge of the lot so he'd know how to get back to it.

His guide store was nowhere in sight.

"I think we have to go to the other side." He tried to swallow, but his throat was so dry from the rising panic that it refused. "That way," he croaked.

Garth jogged toward the left, and Lydia joined him a few seconds later.

"Garth, why can't we go back inside? Wouldn't it be a

lot shorter?"

"Lots," he said. "But my dad would have a conniption if he knew I went toward the sound of guns. That's something he drilled into my brain as a way to avoid criminals in New York." His voice turned deep to mimic his father. "If you hear shooting, run the opposite direction, son."

He'd not only heard gunshots but he had seen the body, so he wasn't going back.

They ran through an area packed with dumpsters and emerged at the front façade of one of the mall's anchor department stores. About ten women did their best impression of a ball of yarn as they tumbled and punched each other by the glass doors of the entrance. It looked like they were fighting for their lives.

Garth hesitated, causing Lydia to brush against his arm.

"What is it?" she asked. "More trouble?"

"Yeah. The place is full of it. Let's go around them." He directed her off the sidewalk to get them away from the violence.

As they ran by, he figured out what it was all about. The women were tugging on upscale merchandise that must have come from the adjacent store. Footwear, purses, and whole outfits fell out of the scrum, only to be grabbed by someone else and brought back into the fight. At the same time, they snarled various low-brow obscenities his dad had instructed him never to use in the company of women. It wasn't a fight for their lives, but they sure acted like it.

"What is that language they're speaking? I don't understand those words."

He glanced her way. "Trust me, you don't need to know them. Do you remember the three numbers? You should only focus on those."

She rattled them off to his satisfaction. He replied with his four numbers.

"Keep running. We aren't stopping for shit."

"You say such disgusting things, Garth," she said with a labored laugh. "I do not need to use a privy."

Her response gave him a moment to appreciate how messed up his life had become. He was with a girl from the mid-1800s. A woman had gotten herself shot in front of him. Others fought over expensive clothing. Hell, a nuclear bomb went off in America.

"I'll teach you more about my language when we have the time. For now—"

A large blue pickup truck with giant mud tires came out of an aisle and turned in front of them, catching him off-guard. Since they were in the middle of the roadway, he had to choose whether to go left or right.

A man stuck his head out of the passenger side. "Out of the street, dumbshits!"

He grabbed Lydia's hand and pulled her to the left, back toward the sidewalk.

The truck belched out black smoke as it rolled by and the driver laid on the horn, which nearly caused Garth to trip on the curb as he hopped onto the walkway.

"Don't run!" the passenger shouted. "No one saw you steal it!" The guy laughed like he enjoyed being in the chaotic scene. A couple of seconds later, Garth heard the man say, "Ladies, ladies, ladies," as the truck stopped next to the fighting women.

There was going to be trouble, but he and Lydia kept running back to the car.

"Why are people so rude in your time?" Lydia inquired from a few paces back.

Garth slowed down after realizing he'd been sprinting

since the truck made them scramble aside. His delay allowed her to catch up.

"These aren't normal folk," he replied.

What would his dad call them? His father read books about situations exactly like this, but Garth couldn't remember if they ever spoke about what to call people acting irrationally during a crisis. Dad's advice usually came down to its most basic: if you get into a disaster situation and people are panicking, don't panic.

The people around the mall could use that advice because they were acting like chickens with their heads cut off.

"They're terrified," he finally explained.

Lydia looked around the parking lot. "But why? There is nothing to be afraid of. No stampeding buffaloes. No bad weather. No river crossing. I don't get it."

"I think it is like an infection. When people get scared, they make other people scared. It spreads to everyone else like a disease. That's why we have to get out of here to somewhere not tainted by fear."

He wondered if there was such a place, but before he could voice the words, he saw a woman sitting on a rock bench at the next corner of the department store.

"Hey, wait up," he said to Lydia before slowing to a walk. "I think she's safe."

The woman held a bundle of blankets at her chest in a motherly way.

"Safe for what?" Lydia asked.

"You'll see," he said with hope.

They walked for a few paces before the woman noticed them. He held up his hands to show he was unarmed. "We don't want to cause trouble, but I really need to use a phone."

"I'm waiting for my husband. He's a police officer." She pointed to the parking lot as if the man had gone to get their car.

"Excellent!" Garth replied. While he experienced unease around the officers and security guards inside the mall, the parking lot absolutely needed some more law and order.

Garth was a few yards from her when he stopped. The woman pulled the swaddled bundle onto her bosom as if Garth was going to try to take it.

"Please. We went into the mall to get my dad's phone number. I only need to borrow your phone for a minute to tell him I'm okay."

Lydia added, "Garth is an honorable man. He and I will watch over you until your husband arrives. Would that be all right?"

He looked at her, pleased to have her endorsement. The woman, however, didn't seem sold.

"My husband is close. He won't be long."

"Can I use your phone until he arrives? Please." He was a second from getting to his knees.

"Fine," the woman said as if he'd worn her down. She pulled out a phone and keyed in the password. "I'm taking it back the second I see my husband."

"Deal!" Garth replied.

He took the phone and repeated those four numbers a few more times, to be sure. After Lydia repeated her three numbers, he had the whole thing.

"Let's do this," he said as he dialed Buck.

While the phone rang, he barely noticed the tornado sirens in the distance.

. . .

I-80, Nebraska

Buck was back on the road, but his heart was gone. It had fallen out of the truck and got run over by all eighteen wheels a few miles back. The asshole on Garth's phone seemed legitimate about killing his son, although he wasn't going to accept it until he saw his son's body. However, it took away all his enthusiasm about heading east.

Connie never took her hand off his thigh. She continued her effort to comfort him. He said nothing, but it meant a lot to experience her caring touch even though he wasn't in the mood to talk about it.

Big Mac also sensed his mood, and he sat between the front seats. Every once in a while, he would paw at Buck's leg as if to mimic the care Connie gave him.

Eventually, he had to recognize it. "You're a good boy."

Belatedly, Buck looked at Connie. "Thank you for being here for me. I want to say something, but I'm so angry and so sad—I really don't know what needs to be said."

"You don't have to say anything, darlin'. I feel the pain you're going through. I've been fighting that feeling since I arrived. The worst part is not knowing."

Buck attacked the steering wheel like he was choking the life out of it. "I know those bastards were lying! You'll see."

"I know," she replied softly.

It was hard to tell if she really believed him, but, to be fair, he couldn't say for sure he believed himself. The last half-hour had seemed like a living nightmare, and he prayed he would wake up before it got any worse.

Buck almost snapped his seatbelt when his phone rang again.

He reached for the phone but looked at the screen before picking it up. It was a number he didn't recognize, and he was most definitely not in the mood to talk to a stranger.

Connie leaned over to look at it. "It says the call is coming from Louisville, Kentucky."

Garth was in Virginia.

"Fuck Kentucky. It's probably a political robocall. That would just fucking figure."

He got angry at the thought of a politician trying to secure his vote while the world fell apart. With his luck, and with everything coming out of the past, he would find himself surrounded by dead politicians. It would be his hell.

"Fuck!" he shouted.

Connie took the phone from the cradle. "May I?"

He was too mad to talk, so he motioned for her to take it. From deep inside the rage, he knew she was attempting to help. If she wanted to deal with a call asking for money to fund some Bluegrass State asshole, so be it.

"Hello?"

She paused for a few seconds.

"Really?" she added.

"Tell them we gave at the office," he said through clenched teeth.

"Really?" she repeated. "Hold on a second."

Connie held the phone toward him. "The call is for you."

"Seriously? I'm not in the mood for bullshit, Connie."

She smiled at him, but there were tears in her eyes.

"What?" he snapped. "Did someone else fucking die?"

It took monumental restraint not to use the F-word a dozen times in each sentence. He wanted to cuss out everyone and everything, but something about her posture made him aware it wasn't the right time for it.

"You take it right now, Buck." She could barely talk.

"Yeah, okay," he said remorsefully.

He gripped the phone, expecting more trauma, but he admitted to himself there was nothing anyone could say on the telephone that would top the bad news he'd already gotten about Garth. Even news of his own death wouldn't make him as sad.

Buck took a deep breath. "Hello?"

TEN

***Search for Nuclear, Astrophysical, and Krono-
metric Extremes (SNAKE). Red Mesa, Colorado***

With the lights back on, Faith stood in front of her team.
They'd been locked in the office and forced to watch a
government film explaining the origins of the secret experiment run out of SNAKE. It had been full of theory and
formulas and was chock-full of implications for changing
the world, but her people seemed most concerned with the
ever-morphing scientist behind the lead plate.

The physics people and computer technicians
peppered her with questions.

"Please!" she shouted. "One at a time." She pointed at
Bob, which she realized an instant too late probably made
her seem to be favoring him.

He stood up. "Thank you, Doctor Sinclair." He looked
around the room. "You all know me. Some of you know this,
but I want to get this out in the open for the rest of you. I
was aware of all this before we launched the Izanagi test."

A few of his peers gasped.

"CERN and SNAKE worked together to duplicate

what you just saw on those two small colliders. There are obviously some similarities to how the new experiment played out compared to the original attempt, but I think this film is a roadmap for how we can power down our collider and free ourselves of this entanglement. I think that's why they showed us this data."

A woman at the back replied. "Will everything return to normal if we shut it all down, like it did for the man behind the shield?"

Bob glanced at Faith with an uncertain look on his face. For the past several days, she and the team had been debating the pros and cons of a total system shutdown either at SNAKE or at CERN. Since General Smith had said he was taking care of CERN, her sole focus was here in Colorado. However, the more they studied the problem, the less they understood where the power was coming from.

The Four Arrows boxes complicated things even more. She'd been lucky she'd convinced Smith to test the removal of one box before doing all of them, because they discovered the unknown power simply transferred to the other three. When the terrorists had come in with C-4, intent on shutting down the remaining boxes no matter the result, she and General Smith had fought to stop them. That effort had only been successful because Smith had given his life to preserve the last one.

Yet the movie made it pretty clear that things had gone back to normal when the power was shut off. Since the only source of power seemed to come through the last Four Arrows device, it suggested a course of action.

"Will it?" the woman in the back repeated as if Bob had taken too long to answer.

"It will not," a familiar man's voice replied.

Dr. Johnson came into the room, causing a stir.

"Traitor!" someone shouted. Others stood up and talked over each other.

He appeared calm as he strode toward Faith. She stepped aside since he was obviously there to address them all.

"Settle," he said, holding his hands up.

After a few more insults from the crowd, they finally began to restore order. Everyone sat back down, save Faith.

"I thought you were at CERN?" she asked when it was quiet.

"I was," he began, "until the end of the experiment. My team and I left the control room at the cusp of the critical final phase. A strange burst of blue energy followed us through the main door and interacted with the control boards. I saw it the instant it happened; it was a total system redline. I pushed the emergency shutdown, but it didn't respond."

Dr. Johnson cupped his hands over his nose and mouth like he was suddenly feeling stressed and didn't want to breathe the air. "The energy wasn't deadly, like electricity, but it did have an effect on us. I watched several members of my team fall to the floor. Eventually, I did as well. However, when I woke up, you'll never guess where I was."

"Here," Bob deadpanned.

"How did you know that?" Dr. Johnson asked while nodding.

Faith interjected. "This is Dr. Stafford."

"Doctor Stafford!" The other scientist beamed. "It's nice to put a face to the name."

Several members of the audience grumbled because it was clear Bob and Dr. Johnson had worked together behind everyone's backs.

Bob seemed uncomfortable. "Well, it hasn't been a

badge of honor over here. Your people don't seem to like me, either." He pointed to his broken nose before continuing. "To your point, the Four Arrows project was designed to transmit data across the planet, so it only makes sense you got caught up in it somehow."

"Bingo." Dr. Johnson pointed to the wall where the movie had played. "You saw it transmit the laser as part of the initial experimentation. Using that laser, we could have introduced gaps in the beams to tap out a Morse code message if we wanted. The idea of transmitting data was solid. What we did not expect was that the powered system would also pick up matter. Organized matter, to boot."

"Organized matter?" a man from the audience asked.

"Me, to be exact. One minute I was at CERN, and the next minute I was lying in pine needles in the forest above us." He pointed to the ceiling. "It's a good thing I landed where I did, too. I could have appeared a thousand feet above the ground, or a thousand below it. I might have appeared in the middle of Highway 85 to the east, or anywhere inside the circle formed by the collider ring."

Faith's sympathy quotient was low for those people who had manipulated her and SNAKE's equipment, but getting dropped on the busy north-south highway at the border of her collider would be a nightmare she wouldn't wish on anyone.

"Why didn't you come in here when you arrived?" Faith inquired. "You could have saved us a lot of trouble in those first hours. Maybe you could have warned us that there would be a terrorist attack."

Dr. Johnson smiled. "I have bosses, like you do. I found a phone and called in, and they sent a helicopter and flew me to their headquarters in Montana. It took a couple of days, but we've been planning to come to your rescue. You're welcome."

Faith wasn't impressed. She didn't fully trust that he'd come from CERN in the way he said, nor did she like his chummy attitude with Bob. It was like he didn't share any of the responsibility for what he'd done to the world.

"That's all great. I'm happy for you. Now, tell us how to fix this fucking mess you've created."

The man turned stoic. "I thought you'd never ask."

Red Mesa, CO

Phil had spent considerable time in combat, so the gunfire by itself wasn't his worry. It was the frightened look on the soldier firing the rifle.

"Stop right there!" the guard screamed.

Phil had been prodding him hard to get his full attention, but he'd gone a little too far with it, so now he put his hands up and stood stock-still.

The second guard put away his radio and joined his partner in aiming a rifle at Phil and Airman Sanchez.

The first guard walked toward Phil. "Say another word, and you're going to regret it." He pulled out some giant zipties, designed to secure prisoners.

A man to Phil's left whistled. He and Sanchez knew what it meant, so they slowly sank to the ground. The guards turned toward the sound, which was exactly what was supposed to happen.

The lead guard was fearless. "Who is that? Identify yourself!"

A second man whistled to the right of the guards.

The guards spun around, which made Phil plant his face in the pine needles. This was the most dangerous part of their gamble. His split team wouldn't shoot directly across the path and hit each other in a crossfire, but every rifle inside of fifty yards belonged to the US Army. If he got hit, it would be classified as friendly fire.

Ethan called out. "You are surrounded. You have ten rifles trained on each of you. Drop your weapons. We're U-S-fucking-Army."

Phil heard the guards mumble to each other, then drop their weapons. By the time he raised his head, Ethan's team was all over the men. The white zip-ties went on the wrists of the two guards.

Ethan spoke as he handed Phil his weapon. "Nice ruse, making them believe you were a lost loud asshole."

The tension of almost getting shot slowly ebbed away from Phil. Much like his near-death experience with the Taliban soldier during the sneak-attack at Bagram, all he could think about was the stuff in his mind when he almost ate a bullet. "I figured you'd shoot each other across the pathway."

"This isn't my first snatch-and-grab," the officer replied more seriously.

Phil looked to a familiar face in the men Ethan had with him. "Corporal Grafton!"

"Nice to see you, sir. The trip here was a bag of dicks, but it was all good training."

"Is your radio working? I could really use it."

Grafton had it strapped on his back, but he didn't appear happy. "No, it's wasted. Not sure how, though."

Phil didn't want to hold up the whole operation. "We'll talk more later."

He waited a few seconds for Ethan to speak.

"Good effort, men. Now let's get these two into the woods."

When Ethan pushed at the back of the first captive, he refused to move.

"We can't go that way," the guard said dramatically.

Ethan gave him a less-friendly shove. "I saw you call this in. We're getting you out of here, so you'll go where I tell you."

"No!" The guard fell to the ground like he'd fainted. "I can't go there! Take me in any other direction."

Ethan and Phil exchanged bemused looks.

"What is it about that way?" Phil asked.

The guard whispered. "It's too close to the edge."

"The edge? The edge of what?" Phil looked in the direction they'd intended to go. It appeared to be pine forest, like everywhere else in the foothills above SNAKE. There were no edges or cliffs within view.

"Just trust me; you don't want to go there, either. There are no guards this way. I swear!" Although his hands were bound, he pointed in the opposite direction.

Ethan wasn't swayed. "No guards? Nice try." He tried to lift the man, but he screamed.

"Dammit, guy! All we're doing is getting you away from the exit door before backup arrives, so we don't have to hurt anyone."

Phil shared the frustration of his CO. It wasn't common practice to casually talk to a prisoner like they were doing, but they were theoretically on the same team, so protocol was vague. They weren't going to hurt a fellow soldier of the United States military, but they had to be sure what they were dealing with before handing themselves over to whoever was in charge at SNAKE.

The mission came first.

Ethan nodded to Phil, his message clear. They picked

up the two men from the ground and dragged them deeper into the forest in the direction the guard feared.

"No! No! Help!" the guard screamed.

Phil searched for material to gag them, but they were traveling light.

Minutes later, the lead guard got even worse.

"I can't go that way! I don't want to disappear! Do you hear me? We're going to disappear. Poof!" He struggled against the men restraining him. Phil managed to hold onto his prisoner as they went along, but the guy broke free and threw an arm around a tree.

"Fuck," Ethan said with exasperation. "How did this guy make it into the military? Such a baby."

That got the guard's attention. "I only want to live; can't you see? If you leave the property of this base, you are going to cease to exist when the experiment is over. That was what they told us back at HQ. That's why we can't let anyone inside, even assholes like you who claim to be US military."

"Hold up," Phil said, amused. "If we walk outside the supercollider under our feet, we're going to disappear?" After teleporting across the planet, he was open to the idea of it, but they were in pristine woodlands, not surrounded by modern equipment like they had been when they'd disappeared from CERN. How could it possibly work in a forest?

The guard nodded. "That's what they told us. They also said there were no other units within five hundred miles, so you can't be who you say you are."

"No units?" Phil mumbled. That part might be true. The remnants of Task Force Blue 7 weren't even on the right continent. He gave another look at the man's unit patch, suddenly realizing it wasn't anything he recognized.

"I told you I was with the 75th Rangers. Care to tell me what unit you're with?" He pointed to the circular blue patch on the guard's shoulder. It looked like a lizard or a snake with a small pair of wings.

The guard warily looked him over, then sighed. "If I tell you, do you promise to not put me outside the ring? You can shut me up or torture me if you must, but please don't make me disappear from existence."

Phil raised his eyebrows. "Sure. We'll go a different direction and keep you inside the ring."

"Keep us *all* in the ring," the guard emphasized. "I'm saving your lives."

"So you keep telling us," Ethan replied skeptically.

"Are we good?" Phil asked.

"Yes, thank God, and thank you," the guard replied with a satisfying sigh. "I'm with the 130th Infantry Division."

Phil and Ethan passed the same doubtful look to each other. It confirmed in Phil's mind what he already knew from seeing the unusual shoulder patch.

There was no such unit in the US Army.

I-80, Nebraska

Buck took the phone from Connie. "This is Buck."

"Dad! I can't believe it's really you. Me and Lydia had to look up your cell phone number in this mall. We saw a lady get shot. A nuke was dropped in Las Vegas! We—" Garth rambled on for another half a minute faster than Buck had ever heard his son speak in the past. He had a ton to say. However, it took Buck about that long to register that the voice on the other end was real.

"Garth! You're alive!" Buck glanced at Connie; her tears now made sense.

"Yeah, of course," Garth answered in a slower cadence. "Why would you think I was dead?"

"I talked to a couple of men who have your phone. They said they killed you during a robbery."

"Oh, yeah." Garth laughed. "You'll never believe what happened to me. I was filling up the car and went in to pay, and then—" He rambled almost as fast as a cattle auctioneer as he described another part of their adventure.

Satisfied he was talking to his living, breathing son, Buck almost broke into tears again. His need to see the lines of the road ahead was the only reason he didn't.

"Garth, I can't tell you how happy I am to hear your voice. This is the best day of my life."

His son laughed as if totally unaware of the emotional wasteland Buck had come through. "Glad I could bring you such joy. We—" Another voice interrupted Garth on his end. The sound became muffled before getting back to normal. "Dad, I have to go. I'm borrowing this nice lady's phone, and her husband is pulling his truck up to us. The mall is like a war zone."

Panic rose in Buck's chest. It was a real possibility he'd never hear his son's voice again. "Garth, listen. We're still coming to you. Where are you?"

"Louisville, Kentucky. At a mall. I saw the name, but I don't remember it."

Buck pressed the phone against his ear as if he were adamant that his son listen to him.

"That's not important. You are on Interstate 64 like we discussed. Good job. Keep going west. We're still on I-80, but we're heading south to get on the 64. I don't have a map in front of me, but I think we'll meet somewhere between Kansas City and St. Louis."

Connie pulled out the road atlas, but he didn't think they'd have time for that.

Shouting came from Garth's end.

"Dad, I have to go! I'll meet you at Kansas City." There was obviously a scuffle going on.

"Meet at the Blue Springs McTruckStop! Blue Springs." They both shared a love of the Golden Arches, and there were giant billboards advertising the place for a hundred miles on either side of it. No one could miss the location.

Several voices came through the phone line at the same time.

"Garth?" he shouted.

The confused jumble of noises continued, but his son's voice broke through. "Blue Springs McDonald's, Dad. I heard you! I'm Oscar Mike!"

The line went dead.

ELEVEN

Louisville, KY

"I'm Oscar Mike!" Garth shouted to his dad a second before the phone was snatched from his fingers. His dad would be proud of him for remembering the Marine slang for "on the move," and he was glad he'd had the time to say it.

"Get your ass over here, Margaret!" a man screamed from a truck parked at the curb.

"I told you I have to go!" the woman shrieked. "My husband made it!"

Tornado sirens screamed in the distance, which seemed to mainline fear into the woman.

"I'm sorry," Garth answered. "I had to tell my dad where we are going to meet." He wasn't sorry he had done it. Not really. The woman was only being unreasonable because her husband had arrived to pick her up.

She clutched her baby in one arm and the phone in the other, but in her rush to stand up and get out of there, the infant fell out of her arms.

"No!" the woman screamed.

Garth reacted with cat-like reflexes crafted over years of video gaming. He dove sideways and slid under the tumbling tot. A microsecond before the bundle of joy smacked the concrete walkway, he got his hands under it for the save.

"Gotcha!" He huffed after the tremendous explosion of energy.

Despite the grab, the baby weighed a lot more than he'd expected, and he scraped his forearms on the ground during the catch. They lit up like brushfires once he realized what he'd done.

"What the hell! Leave her alone!" the man in the truck yelled through the open window.

"I've got her baby," Garth replied half-heartedly. His excitement at saving a child seeped away when he got a look at the baby's face. "I think..."

There was no kid. The wrapped blankets held a treasure trove of allergy medication and packets of razor blades.

"What the hell?" On his knees, he still held the bundle as if it were a living thing. "Where's your baby?"

The woman turned ugly. "There is no baby, you idiot. We're taking this shit. Give it back!" She snatched the contraband from Garth's arms. He let it go because he wasn't sure what had happened.

He finally noticed Lydia tugging at his arm to get him to stand.

"Garth, let's continue to your tack-see." She glanced over her shoulder at the nearby truck.

It made more sense when he stood up and watched the woman open the door of her escape vehicle. She tossed the swaddled treasure onto the floorboard and hopped in after it.

"Oh," he said like he'd been missing a practical joke until that moment.

The woman looked his way as her husband put the truck in gear. "You two should get while the getting's good. The world is falling apart." She signed off by flipping them the bird as the truck sped away.

"That was unnecessary. I tried to help." Garth didn't take it personally, but it bothered him he'd endangered himself to help someone so undeserving.

Lydia got him moving. "Come on, let's go. I thought you did great, Garth. If it had been a real baby, you would be a hero."

"I guess we can't trust anyone out here. Not really."

"You trust me, don't you?" she asked as they jogged farther around the perimeter of the mall.

He had to speak up, because another tornado siren began its wail, this time a lot closer than the others. "You are the only person I trust, so yeah."

She seemed satisfied with his answer. "If you tell me what to look for, I can help keep watch for bad guys. I helped Pa by looking out for coyotes and foxes back on the wagon train, although the truth of it is there wasn't much else to do most days."

"Watch for everyone," he replied darkly. "Anyone can be a bad guy, I guess. That faker proved it."

"I'll try," she said like she meant it.

After another minute of jogging, he saw the taxi out on the lot. Its horrible paint job made it stand out from a hundred yards away. Most of the cars had already abandoned the parking area, so it sat alone.

"That way!" he commanded.

They left the sidewalk and made their way into the parking spaces of the huge lot. While they ran, he tried to think of what his dad would say to Lydia. What was the best way to tap into her skillset while running and driving through cities filled with women willing to fake holding babies so they could steal razor blades?

They got to the taxi without any interference. Cars and trucks piled up at the exits and jostled around each other with horns blaring, but they were far across the lot from his car.

"You need a gun, Garth. If we were traveling in the wild back home, my pa would insist on it."

Because you can't carry a cop with you. It was one of his dad's jokes.

He reappraised her. "Your dad and mine would have been good friends. I'm sure of that. My dad would be pissed if I was out here with no weapon, and by the way, he taught me to never call them guns. It was advice from his Marine days, I think. Anyway, do you think I should carry the rifle around with me?"

Garth patted the trunk because the lone rifle case was in there.

"I don't know," she said, biting her lip. "Maybe keep it out when we are on the highway? Out there, we won't have the protection of those lawmen we saw inside your mall."

After checking that there was no one lurking close by, he opened the trunk and pulled out one of his dad's AR-15s. He slammed the trunk, then rushed the black rifle around the side of the car and tossed it on the backseat.

"Okay, get in. We're out of here!" Garth slid into the driver's seat a second after Lydia shut her door.

It took twenty minutes to get out of the parking lot. He maneuvered the car toward the others at the nearest exit, but he kept a good distance between him and the main pack of anxious horn-blowers. It meant he was delayed getting out, but he didn't want to risk riding someone's bumper and getting into an argument. If things got bad, he was ready to reach into the back seat and get the gun, but he wanted to avoid trouble, not find it.

Once he was back on I-64, he released some of the tension in the knot around his stomach, but the danger was far from over, and he was already worn out. "Hey, Lydia, I have two jobs for you."

She pulled her leg onto the seat as she turned to him. "I'm ready for anything."

He smiled. "Yeah, that's good. Be ready. I also want you to talk to me. Tell me about your days back on the wagon train. Talk to me about your home. Anything to keep me chatting back, so I don't fall asleep."

"I can do that. What else?"

"If we do run into trouble on the highway, I won't be able to drive and get the gun at the same time. You're going to have to reach back there and get it for me. Maybe...well, you might have to shoot it." He couldn't imagine things getting so desperate, but if he had learned nothing else from his always-prepared father, he knew to assume things were going to be the worst.

"I said I'm ready, Garth. I mean it. My life wasn't very exciting until I met you, but let me think of what to talk about ..."

He listened to her attentively but kept his eyes on the rearview mirror, and he didn't fully exhale until the tornado sirens of Louisville were far behind. It had helped a lot to hear his dad's voice and have a plan of action for where to meet, but it wasn't enough.

One more check in the mirror—still no mushroom cloud over the city.

Garth took his left hand off the steering wheel for a

moment. It shook like a leaf on a windy day, and it wasn't because of the air blowing in through the broken window. There was nothing concrete to fear at that instant, but it seemed like there was an underlying tension and fear he couldn't quite shake.

Be strong for Lydia.

He casually put his hand back on the wheel, then glanced at his pioneer friend to determine if she'd seen it. Thankfully, she was busy keeping watch and talking about her life like they were sitting around a campfire.

She seemed unaffected by all they'd gone through.

In his mind, he believed he was pulling Lydia through the collapse of his modern world. He'd made decisions that had saved their lives and gotten them out of some sticky situations. However, her stalwart resolve and lack of fear made him realize she was equally important in their two-person team. He didn't want to let her down. Ever.

Be strong with *Lydia.*

I-80, Nebraska

Buck drove along the straightest stretch of interstate in America, which had endless flat fields on each side, but he took it in like he was on the most scenic, curve-ridden, interesting highway in all of North America.

Garth is alive.

He couldn't stop thinking about it. Each mile was one additional hurdle that brought him closer to his son. His natural love of driving blossomed as he feathered the wheel, and even the threat of blacking out again couldn't dampen his spirits. He hummed a few bars of *The Marines' Hymn* for good measure.

"I'm so happy for you, Buck." Connie shared his enthusiasm, but he knew there was one remaining thorn in her side.

"Yeah, life is great right now. And don't worry. We've got luck on our side. Garth is okay , and we're going to find your son too. I just know it!"

He really did feel like he could take on the world.

"I know it too," she replied. "But we still have other problems out there. The radio hasn't said anything more about those bombs. What do you make of that?"

They'd been driving east for an hour since Garth had called, and the whole time they'd been listening to the radio for news about nuclear war. However, reports were still unclear about where the bombs had hit, and they said nothing about who'd dropped them. If he'd had time to think it over, he would have directed Garth to meet him somewhere less populated than Kansas City, but he had done the best he could under the circumstances.

Garth is alive. That's all that matters.

"As long as the war stays in the Southwest, we have a chance." Of all the states it could have been, he hated that hers was targeted, but for the moment, it worked in their favor.

"I'm sure everything is going to work out. No one is really dumb enough to start a war when the rest of the planet is having all these ...problems." She stopped talking when a black shape caught their attention up ahead.

"Bring it on!" he declared. "I'm ready for anything."

Connie laughed a little. "Don't tempt fate, Buck. I'm sure God or fate or Mother Nature can dish out more than we can take."

"I know I shouldn't overdo it, but I can't stop shouting to the rooftops about Garth. You'll know the feeling soon enough, I promise."

It was his turn to reach over and touch her arm. "Are you good?" he asked softly.

She brightened back to her old self. "I will be. We only have to get past whatever is about to come our way."

The highway didn't have a kink in it, so they stared down the four lanes of pavement to the growing mass of flying creatures. Unlike the spreading darkness associated with the wayward aircraft carrier, this new threat rose and fell like waves. As they closed the distance, he was able to make some guesses about what they were.

"Starlings." He pointed ahead. The gyrations of the swarm were exactly like the flocks of birds he'd often see while driving. The only difference was the size. These birds filled the sky to the east with inky, fast-moving blotches.

"I've never seen that many in one place," Connie replied.

Big Mac, as was his way when tension rose inside the cab, started to whine.

Connie reached under the dashboard to pet him. "It's okay, little guy. Buck and I will keep you safe. It's just a bunch of birds."

In the grassy median, a dozen or so lanky antelope hoofed it away from the approaching mass. The deer-like animals seemed unaware of the vehicles passing on each side of them.

"They seem frightened," Connie remarked.

The cab became quiet as they peered ahead at the freak of nature, but after a few more miles, Buck began to doubt his first guess.

Small insects pelted the windshield, forcing him to use the wipers to remove the goopy messes they left. When it happened a few more times, he made the connection.

"Those aren't birds..."

Connie picked up on it right away. "They're locusts."

"Oh, shit," Buck exclaimed. He'd driven through any number of small swarms of bugs over the years, sometimes requiring the time-consuming cleaning of his radiator grille. However, he'd never seen anything like what was up ahead.

"There are some birds," Connie remarked as she pointed out her window. "They're going the wrong way, though."

Hundreds of birds flew west, away from the arriving swarm of insects. A hawk crossed in front of him as he watched, nearly striking his windshield.

"Those birds are scared shitless."

Connie still looked out her window. "Should we follow their lead? I know we have to go east, then south. Maybe we should go south, then east?"

He didn't have a lot of time to make up his mind, so he slowed the convoy.

"Grab the atlas. We can see if there's a way out. I'll contact the others on the CB and let them know we're thinking of making a turn."

She chuckled as she felt around next to her seat for the book of maps. "I don't think they're going to complain."

Faced with another challenge, and busy with mics and maps and driving, he still went back to the only thing that mattered to him.

Garth is freaking alive!

TWELVE

Search for Nuclear, Astrophysical, and Krono-metric Extremes (SNAKE). Red Mesa, Colorado

"The way to fix this, as Dr. Sinclair so succinctly put it, is to blow up the experiment."

Faith replied because everyone else was silent. "Doctor, we've fought hard to keep this place running. We stopped a terrorist attack that was intent on shutting us down. They could come back at any minute, in fact. Now you say the terrorists had it right?"

She immediately wondered if Dr. Johnson's people had been the terrorists. It seemed incredible, but that was where her mind traveled when nothing else made any sense.

Dr. Johnson spoke with a deep, rich timbre, which added gravitas to his words. "The world as we know it is about to end. That's bad enough, but the real shitter is that none of us can stop it."

She'd been thinking along those lines since the NORAD soldiers had arrived. The genie was out of the bottle, and all the madness in the news couldn't be ignored or reversed. Some level of worldwide chaos and instability was going to be with humanity for a long time. However, she'd never dreamed she'd be asked to give up. "You came here to tell us to hold out our arms and welcome the end?"

The man was short and a little on the pudgy side, but he was a heavyweight in the physics community. He stood in front of Faith's peers and controlled the room.

"Definitely not. We have much to do before the end arrives. That's why I've gathered you here and let you in on the big secret. No matter how badly my bosses want it to be true, the world cannot go on without bringing in all the scientific knowledge we can. General Smith did a noble job of bringing in scientists from all over America. His foresight really helps now."

Faith quietly groaned as she took a seat in one of the empty chairs in the front row. Between multiple bomb blasts, a train accident, and running for her life, her body was exhausted. "Everything we've done has been for nothing? Sir, we've lost people here. Good people."

"And millions, perhaps billions, are slated to die in places outside your cocoon of safety."

"Billions?" she asked with skepticism. "What kind of disaster are we talking about?"

"All of them," he deadpanned. "Right now California is split in two, and the SoCal tectonic plate and everyone on it is heading out to sea. Magma is bubbling up in the Yellowstone caldera as the plates shift, and the geomagnetic field protecting us from the sun's radiation is out to lunch in some places. And that isn't even the bad stuff."

Faith gave him a tell-me-more glance.

He went on. "Two nuclear detonations happened today. One was in the remote desert of New Mexico, and the other happened in the lonely country west of Las Vegas. That is what really has America blinded by the headlights."

Her people freaked out like she'd never seen. Multiple people spoke over each other.

"Be quiet!" she yelled.

They mostly listened.

"Was it an attack?" Faith asked in a tired voice.

"No, not at all." Dr. Johnson seemed surprised. "I can't believe you would even ask such a question. Haven't you figured out what's been happening out there beyond your perfect little circle?"

She nodded. "A little. One of our scientists lost his pacemaker when he left the collider property. Planes have come out of the past. General Smith told us some other things, plus what we've gleaned from the news, but there's so much going on it is hard to know what's true. We've been stuck in here for a very long time, doctor."

"I'm sure that's true, so here are the facts. You've seen the movie I brought, so you have some idea of how things work. Energy flowing between the two supercolliders gains new properties when it taps into the dark energy locked in the rocks under the Earth's surface. It changes reality on the receiving end. As I'm sure you've figured out, the effects are more pronounced on your exponentially larger supercollider here at SNAKE. It isn't just reality that is bent, but also time."

"We've guessed as much," Faith replied. "Are we going to fix it or not?"

"*Can* we fix it?" Bob added from inside the audience.

"One thing at a time," Dr. Johnson responded. "Those bombs were nuclear tests done in the 1940s and '50s. Time has come forward in those places. They weren't new bombs dropped by a hostile power."

Faith expressed disbelief. "How do you know for certain?"

Johnson laughed in what was almost a cackle. "People called it into local newsrooms. We took it from there."

Missy stood up in the middle of the room. "I've been listening to the radio since I started working with all the new scientists. They mentioned a small nuclear attack today, but that was all they said. I didn't hear anything about testing."

"And you won't, not for a long time. Maybe never. Right now, the news reports can only say nuclear explosions were seen in those areas. We aren't telling anyone the truth."

"But why?" Missy pressed. "We can handle it."

"You, maybe. But America the beautiful? No way. We're keeping it as low-key as possible to quell the panic of the nation."

Faith laughed. "How does that help anyone? You have to tell them the truth, so they know we aren't at war."

"Don't worry," Dr. Johnson answered evenly. "We control the news. Didn't you know? Everything that gets said out there is approved by us. Our belief is that it is better to have people think we are at war than to tell them time-traveling nuclear tests have come into the present. It is also why we have a media blackout of what's happening in California. There are a few other oddities we've wallpapered over using our friends in the news media. I'm sure you can see why?"

Missy plopped down into her chair.

Faith didn't know how to respond because it was so far out of her hands.

Dr. Johnson held out his arms and spoke like he was rallying the crowd. "My friends, you are safe. There's nothing to worry about here inside the loop of your beloved collider. That was why we came. That's why we're waiting for others to arrive."

Faith wasn't sure where he was going with his talk, but she was positive she didn't like it.

He continued. "You've been brought in on a dirty little secret, I'm afraid. It pains me to be the one to tell you this, but that bastard Shinano blabbed most of it when he went on television."

"He described SNAKE as a safe place," she said almost to herself.

Dr. Johnson pointed to her. "Yep. We worked hard to paint SNAKE as the bad guy the past few days, but he ruined most of our efforts."

Faith was too tired to express all of her anger, but she let a little go. "Oi! You bastards are why the protesters showed up!"

"Don't blame my bosses or me. We were protecting you."

"That was what General Smith said," she conceded.

"And he was. We were all lucky he was able to get here ahead of the rest of us."

She was going to have to unpick his involvement later.

Dr. Johnson went on. "The villain is Mr. Shinano. He was the backer of this failed effort, but he and his people have now gone totally off the reservation. We believe his company lackeys brought in the C-4 to end their mistake. Still, he was telling the truth. This place is a lifeboat on an ocean of calamity taking place out there. We are doing our best to make sure the *right* people come here while still hitting our quotas, but he threw a giant monkey wrench into this operation."

She was getting frustrated with his lack of clarity. "So, there is a way to stop the disaster? To fix it?"

He looked at the floor as if saddened. "Dark energy has properties we can't identify or control. Now SNAKE and

CERN are like two mule deer with their antlers tangled together after fighting for dominance. If left alone, the two animals might never get free, and they'll die a slow death from starvation. However, my group has enacted a plan to kill one of those deer so the other may live."

Faith suddenly understood his point. "If Shinano was correct, you came here to be safe. That means…"

"CERN must be destroyed."

Sydney Harbor, Australia

Standing at the railing of the boat, Dez was tired and rushed and full of adrenaline, but she'd made up her mind. Her life's mission had been to save animals, and she couldn't allow those inside the truck to remain trapped in there. The *Majestic* might have been pulling away from the pier, but she was prepared to jump across the gap and make things right, even if it meant she was going to miss her trip to America.

"I have to save them," she said to herself.

She took a deep breath of anticipation, fought off her doubts about whether jumping back was the right thing to do, and leaned forward. However, someone grabbed her firmly by the arm before she could do it.

"Zandre? I have to go!"

"I know," he said sadly, "but I can't let you. Not like this."

"But we were responsible for locking them up. They'll die without our help."

Her opportunity to jump frittered away even as she watched. Zandre let her go once the boat was about three meters out. It was much too far to jump.

"Fuck, we can't let them die," she complained. Zandre

had never shown any hint of betrayal in all the years she'd known the older man. This was the first.

"I can't let you die, Dez. Your father and I would do anything for our kids. At least, that was what we told each other before he had you and Faith. I, sadly, never found the right woman to give me one."

She looked at the shore and considered jumping into the water.

Zandre read her mind. "I won't stop you if you want to swim for it. Australia's a big country, as you know. I can't put you in a closet while we sail past her, but know I'd do anything to protect you and get you to safety because of that promise to your father. Hell, I'll jump in with you if you want to go back."

The chugging engine rumbled below her feet, and the vibration grew in intensity as the ship sailed for the narrow harbor exit. That would be the best place to debark if she was really going for it.

"Do you think someone will find them and let them out?" she asked.

Zandre's eyes were sympathetic. "You said we could get to safety by going to America. I put everything I could into this small bag based on what you told me. Whether those animals get out of my truck or not, the world is going to shit, right, mate?" He put his hand on her shoulder in a fatherly manner. "What happens to all the other animals out in the wild when it does? At least ours don't have to worry about being eaten."

It was a poor argument, but Zandre was better suited to being out in the bush than on a debate podium. Still, it served to break down her resolve a little more.

"I really don't know what we're going to find in America. My sister was vague."

"But you believed her?"

"You betcha."

"Then I believe her. Things are disappearing in strange ways. I don't know if this is magic, or aliens, or the work of an evil genius. All I know is I want to get you safe from it. Me too, as it turns out."

They shared a quiet laugh as the boat got well out into the harbor.

"Oi," she said excitedly. "Why don't we ask the captain to radio back to the harbor and ask someone to let the animals out?"

It seemed so obvious.

Zandre smiled. "I don't know why I didn't think of that."

But before he could go to the bridge, she realized how it would be a mistake.

"Wait," she begged. "You can't call it in."

For a moment, she glanced down at the water and considered jumping again.

"Why not, Dez? Your idea is bang-on."

She sighed. "We can't endanger anyone else. What if they send a pregnant woman or an elderly dock worker? They won't know how to handle a Tasmanian Tiger. And who knows what a Duck of Doom would do when it's scared? I can't have that on my conscience."

Zandre patted her on the back. "You think of everyone but yourself. Your father would be proud of you."

She smiled and accepted the compliment, and she did want to avoid getting anyone hurt, but her reluctance to jump and save the animals herself stemmed more from fear than from selflessness.

Dez was afraid of the water.

· · ·

I-80, Nebraska

"There's a cutoff!" Connie cried. It was hard to hear over the sound of locusts beating the front windshield.

"How far?" he asked.

"A few miles," she replied.

The swarm shifted direction before Buck could think about his options. Turning around wasn't what he wanted to do, but the situation was different from the buffalo herd in Wyoming. There were plenty of highways cutting south toward Kansas. They passed one every ten miles, it seemed. However, once the swarm was upon them, it took away his reason to change course, so he ordered the convoy to stick to him like glue, and he'd get them through.

The wipers swished the carcasses out of his view, but a messy film built up that the wiper fluid was unable to clear.

"We have to slow down," he told Connie. Then, on the CB, he said the same thing.

Mac howled in his crate back on the sleeper bed.

"I hear you, buddy. We'll be through this soon."

An impossible number of insects swarmed the truck. Sometimes, the dark shapes became so thick, it was hard to see anything on the highway ahead. It was like driving at night in a blinding rainstorm.

Cutting speed helped reduce the splatter factor, but some of the locusts still fell out of the sky and bashed themselves on the glass, as if they'd decided to kill themselves on the Peterbilt.

The hood was covered with a blanket of bodies two inches thick.

The downpour was nerve-wracking, but Buck tried not to let it get to him. "Hey, Connie. When we get to Kansas City, what do you say we get us some of the best barbecue this side of the Mississippi River?"

The engine growled as Buck downshifted to a lower gear. Not only was it hard to see ahead, but the locusts covered every square inch of the road surface. Aside from the taillights of a car far ahead and a couple of headlights from a truck going the other way, there were no signs of human civilization.

"You've got a screw loose, mister. How can you think of food when we're being greased over by the entrails of a billion bugs?"

He laughed.

"Spend some time in the Marines, and you'll learn to eat no matter what's going on around you. In Iraq, I once ate breakfast next to a sewage lagoon that was—"

"Please, no!" she said with mock horror.

The engine coughed, causing him and Connie to lurch forward.

She became serious again. "What was that?"

Mac yelped as if mirroring her question.

A wave of locusts fell upon them, making it all but impossible to see outside. He didn't want to frighten his passengers, but he was willing to bet his motor's air filter would need to be drained of locust juice.

The wipers worked at full speed to keep the glass clear, but each swipe was less effective than the last. Almost without realizing it, he'd painted himself into a corner. If the truck broke down and they stopped, they might soon be buried under a mountain of dead locusts.

"Just tell me when we reach the turnoff," he replied. "We'll be fine."

THIRTEEN

"I think this trip voids the warranty of my truck," Buck joked as the locusts continued to pile up against his windshield and inside the air intake. He knew the motor better than his own voice, and right now it was talking trash.

He shut off the air conditioner to take some of the load off the engine, and he broke out in a sweat two seconds later.

Connie didn't rise to his humor. "The exit is close. I think I see a sign up ahead."

He saw it too.

"There!" he shouted.

Connie picked up the CB mic. "Guys, we're at the turnoff, thank God. Follow us."

"Roger, Connie," Eve replied. Monsignor also confirmed he was still back there.

She looked at Buck. "We're going to make it."

"Damn right, we are. This trip isn't going to end with a swarm of insects shoveling out our innards, I'll tell you that right now."

"Eww."

Some drivers chose to pull over and park with their hazard lights on, but Buck wasn't one to sit out a battle. Plus, he worried the crawling critters would have time to further investigate the engine compartment and get where they could do real damage. He figured their best chance was to keep going.

He was already moving at walking pace, so the exit ramp up to the intersecting highway was easy to handle. Despite the insane number of locusts and the darkness they created, Buck used the fence lines along the edge of the roadway as a guide. He followed them as he might during a whiteout snowstorm.

"Turning right," Connie relayed to the others.

As Buck gave it some gas, the rain-like sound of insects crashing on his windshield kicked up again. The wiper fluid wasn't rated for constant hard use like this, and the wipers mostly swished the bug guts from side to side, so he had to use a sliver of clean-ish glass on the outer edge. There were splats of bug juice there as well, but they hadn't been smooshed around.

"It's a good thing I'm not afraid of bugs," Connie said matter-of-factly.

"I thought all girls were afraid of them." Buck reached over and poked her side to show he was being silly. He wanted to make sure neither of them succumbed to the gloom outside.

"Not in my family. I had two older brothers, and they would have tortured me if they knew I was afraid of bugs or other animals. When they played with worms, so did I. When they went out hunting, I did, too. One day I realized I wasn't putting on an act. I really did enjoy being out in nature."

"You liked going into the *au natural*," he said as if fondly remembering being outside.

"I don't believe that means what you think it means." She laughed.

"In nature, right?"

Connie giggled like a schoolgirl. "It means being naked, Buck."

He acted surprised. "Even better!"

She rolled her eyes. "Kiss a man, and the next thing you know he's talking about being *au natural*."

"Well, this isn't how I pictured our first date, you know?" He gestured outside. "The sun is gone. Bug juice is bleeding through the dashboard. That nonstop crunch under the tires won't go away. I hoped to do better."

"Keep trying, mister. This is not a first date. You'll have to wait for something a little more impressive for this girl."

He headed the Peterbilt south along the two-lane road for a few minutes while he got his bearings. The road was piled inches high with locusts, so there was no seeing the painted lines of the lanes, but the fences on each side of the road once again gave him his landmarks. All he needed to do was keep it between them.

The radio had been spotty inside the swarm, but it came back on now. "Once again, Cornhusker listeners are reminded of the nearest SNAKE-approved emergency response locations. Lincoln. North Platte. Omaha. If you have started your journey to Denver, Colorado, please turn around and head to those locations. You will be safe from the ongoing crisis."

Buck brushed his sweat-soaked forehead with the back of his hand. "Damn, they must have figured out that not everyone could get to Denver. It was insane of them to close all those highways. Some dumb-ass probably got fired for that fiasco."

The highways around Denver had been shut down yesterday, but the news had nothing about them today. He assumed that meant they were now open.

"It all feels wrong," she complained. "What is it about those towns that is going to protect people from all this?" She pointed outside.

"Mega-sized bug zappers?" he suggested.

"I'm serious, Buck. The radio is sending people to these locations, but what good are they going to be? How will they protect us from disaster after disaster? They won't protect anyone from a nuclear attack, either. Bugs aside, they should be setting up relief shelters in the middle of these fields, far from cities. No one will nuke a field."

"I don't know. I guess when we get to Garth, we'll see if there is a better option than that lab in Denver." He had his heart set on going to SNAKE, but he still had a lot of ground to cover, so he was going to withhold his final decision until it was time to make the call.

"Holy shit," Connie exclaimed. "It's getting lighter."

Mac came out of his crate and wagged his tail so fiercely his rear legs bounced.

"I swear you can speak English," Buck said to his Golden buddy.

"Maybe he sees the light, too." Connie leaned forward and tried to find a clear spot on her side of the windshield. "We all feel it."

"Things are getting better," he said hopefully.

"It's doing something out there, for sure."

"Then let's take advantage of it." He tested his luck by giving the big rig a little more gas. As long as the intake wasn't totally clogged, he could get down the road.

The flat fields were blanketed solid with the hopping little monsters, but the skies to the south weren't as filled with them.

Ten minutes later, even those on the ground had thinned out.

"Geez, look at that." Connie's attention was on her side mirror.

He peered into his. The black swarm filled most of the sky behind them, but the top of the ominous black cloud lit up like a strobe light.

"A bug thunderstorm," he said with awe.

Soon he saw the lines of the road again.

Buck put the hammer down and waited to see if the big diesel could handle it. After listening with satisfaction for a few seconds, he tried the next most important piece of equipment on his Peterbilt.

Once the air conditioner was back on, he let out a huge sigh of relief.

"We're back in business!"

East St. Louis, IL

"You are going to love this," Garth said to Lydia.

He had made good time on the interstate once they got out of Louisville. The number of cars on the road had declined drastically, and he suspected it was because the radio kept talking about safe cities—places the scared population could go to save themselves from the threat of bombs, hurricanes, and other phenomena plaguing the United States. Oddly enough, none of them were on I-64.

Terra Haute, Indiana. Bowling Green, Kentucky. Cairo, Illinois.

He'd seen road signs for those cities, but none of them

were on the way. Not that he cared, however. He wasn't going to go anywhere for safety until he made it to his dad in Kansas City.

Garth drove the taxi over a giant bridge into downtown St. Louis.

"You were right," Lydia told him. "This is much larger than Louisville."

He chuckled. "No, that's not why I wanted you to see this. These are tiny towns compared to my home in New York City. I wanted you to see the Gateway Arch. We learned about it in social studies. It was built to commemorate pioneer settlers like you."

"Really? We were important enough to get an arch?"

"You were. Uh, are." From the bridge, they had a perfect view of the riverfront along the Mississippi River and the skyscrapers of the city behind it. The Arch was supposed to be right on the river, he thought. "But I don't know why we can't see it."

She strained to look over the side of the bridge. "Is it down there? I see a lot of boats on the water."

He tried to see what she was looking at, but a tall, circular building got in his way as he drove. The Riverside Hotel was about thirty stories tall, and it blocked the riverfront.

"Awe, I missed them," he replied. "Wait! I see now." As they passed the end of the hotel, but before they went into the city, he got a brief glimpse of hundreds of steam paddle-boats down on the water. They looked like long john donuts with spinning paddles at the back. Twin stacks belched out black smoke from the tops of those boats that were on the move.

"The Arch should have been visible as we drove across the bridge. It was built to be higher than the whole city. It's gone." It reminded him of the numerous time issues he'd seen the past few days. The problem was in St. Louis, too. "This city ain't right."

A sign welcomed them to the Show Me State.

"I've been to Missouri!" she said with excitement before tempering it a bit. "I was here in St. Louis a few months ago, but it didn't look anything like it does today..."

He supposed she felt like she'd come full circle, but he could only imagine what it would be like to visit the same city a hundred and fifty years apart.

"Hey," he said enthusiastically. "Look at that sign. It says Kansas City is in this direction."

He was distracted by showing her the road sign when two white police cruisers passed them like they were chasing the most dangerous fugitives in America. The fast-moving vehicles made the wind howl like a demon through his broken window.

He jerked the wheel out of instinct.

"Shit!"

He didn't come close to losing control of the car, but he did swerve. Before he fully regained his bearings, two regular cars passed him traveling almost as fast as the police.

"It's like a pursuit in reverse," he remarked.

"Those police are being chased?" she asked.

"I guess. I don't know." He gave the car more gas. "What I do know is that the police aren't going to pull anyone over who is behind them. Maybe we can kick it up a notch."

He'd been doing close to the speed limit the entire time on the highway because he didn't want to get pulled over with a gun in the backseat, but this gave him an incentive to break the rules.

As they drove across the city of St. Louis, several more

police cars joined the first two. Once, a car came up behind him with lights flashing, and Garth thought he'd blown his whole trip, but once he moved out of the way, the police vehicle sped by. By the time they left suburban St. Louis, there was a procession of ten police cars up ahead.

"Garth, this feels unsafe."

The wind noise made it seem like they were doing two hundred miles per hour, but he wasn't going much over a hundred. Nonetheless, it was dangerously fast for a driver without a license, and the open window amplified the fear factor.

"I've got this. If we stick with the police, we can go as fast as they do. Look, these other cars are sticking with them, too. I'm sure they'll get pulled over before we do." He had no idea if that was true, but it helped him justify the newfound speed streak in him.

"Well, I trust you." She held onto her seatbelt like it was a security blanket. He felt bad for her, but there was no chance he'd give up his good luck. The Arch was missing, so the weird stuff with time was everywhere. The option to play it safe was long gone.

"We have half a tank of gas, a six-pack of Mountain Dew, and a breezy howl we can't turn off." He pointed to his busted window. "Nothing can stop us now!" He stifled a yawn after he spoke, noting to himself it seemed weird that he would be tired when there was so much excitement happening right then.

Lydia seemed to settle down when she saw him in control. It was his interpretation, at least. He did his best to project confidence now that he saw how close they were to the end.

Dad and I might already be in the same state.

FOURTEEN

***Search for Nuclear, Astrophysical, and Krono-
metric Extremes (SNAKE). Red Mesa, Colorado***

"General Smith said he had a team shutting things
down at CERN. We were waiting for the results of that
mission when he and I ...went into the tunnels. He didn't
come out, and his people wouldn't talk to me after he was
dead."

Faith was happy to find out that SNAKE wasn't the
target, but there was a team of fellow scientists sitting in
Europe at that moment who had huge targets on their
backs.

"I only know what I was told by my bosses. The mission
departed Ramstein yesterday afternoon and made it to
Geneva last night. However, we have no idea what
happened once they got there. We've been trying to raise
them ever since, but America is in full retreat from the
European theater. Most of our satellites are gone, and
communications are a nightmare."

"So they might still succeed?" she pressed. "We have to
call CERN immediately."

Dr. Johnson slowly shook his head, as if he'd thought about it but had come to a negative conclusion. "Energy is still coming through to the last Four Arrows container. We know CERN is up and running based on that evidence, so the mission failed."

"What if—"

He interrupted her. "It won't matter, Doctor. Even if they shut off the local electrical power, it won't break the connection to us."

"How can you possibly know that?" she asked.

"Dr. Sinclair, I know the CERN campus better than almost anyone. I was there when the experiment was engaged. I was part of the world's first matter teleportation. Whatever trickle of electricity comes out of that station, it is secondary to the dark energy tethered to it through the Earth's mantle. The only way to stop the energy transfer is to destroy CERN down to the foundation."

"How?" Bob asked.

"Nukes."

"Sheesh," Bob replied. "Seems like overkill."

"The military strategists tell me they can't be sure a conventional explosion will do enough damage to the entire thirty-two-kilometer ring. We have to be sure everything is gone so there will be no chance of any energy making its way into the virtual corridor created between them and us."

"And you trust the military to get it done?" Faith asked sadly.

"I trust them with my life. They have an entire division of troops protecting the last Four Arrows box in your facility. It's also a key element for making the destruction of CERN a success."

"That doesn't make any sense."

"General Smith saved your precious hardware, Dr.

Sinclair. Our testing suggests losing the last box would have made the time dilation and schisms worse out in the world, but even more than that, it would have meant we'd have to change our tactics and try to nuke SNAKE instead of CERN. If that had happened, you and I would have been out of luck for surviving this disaster."

"Because you would have had to go to CERN." It was Donald Perkins.

"Ah, nice to see you are still with us, Doctor," Dr. Johnson replied. "And yes, the two-deer-fighting-for-dominance thing was accurate. It's either them or us."

Donald chuckled. "Do you think it's possible the Europeans might have sent someone to blow us up? You know, so they don't have nukes raining down on a city smack in the middle of their territory?"

She noticed a disturbing emotion pass over Dr. Johnson's face.

"No, that's madness. No one knows about this..."

Faith didn't think he was at all convincing.

"Well, I, um, must leave you for a bit. The guards outside have orders to watch over you as a group until we can figure out what to do with you. I'm sorry I can't offer anything more, but I must do as the Army says too."

"Doctor, you know this isn't right. None of it. You are at least going to warn people at CERN, aren't you? They need to get clear of the bomb."

He walked to the door. "You have to think of this as a necessary evil. If we give them any warning, European security services may catch wind, and their armies might retaliate. Imagine going to war with Europeans over something that is destined to save humanity? Better to have one nuclear smudge in Switzerland than hundreds across America, right?"

Dr. Johnson opened the door and nodded to a guard outside. Before he left, he turned back around to face the unsettled scientists in conference room five. "Trust me, we've looked at every option. You'll thank me when everything goes back to normal."

Before anyone could reply, he started on a different topic. "They tell me you can go in groups to the cafeteria and the restrooms, but the guards will stick with you. The rest of your group, as well as the scientists brought in by NORAD, will remain in the main auditorium."

Missy stood up. "Can I go back down there? I was helping them before you brought me here."

"It isn't really up to me, but I'll try. Come on." He waved her over.

Faith's assistant walked across a row and went right to her. "I'm sorry I can't stay here," she said sadly. Missy hugged her while whispering in her ear, "I can tell you want to warn CERN. I'll try to find a way."

"Thank you," she whispered back.

Watching her old friend go out the door was the inspiration for her to find her own way to resist the takeover by the military. Dr. Johnson might be in control of SNAKE, and the military might be swarming over every inch of their lab, but there was no reason to give up on her fellow human beings. She had no illusions about stopping a nuclear attack, but there had to be a way to at least warn the victims.

I know just the person.

Red Mesa, CO

"Tell me what the hell is going on here? What is this bullshit about disappearing?"

Ethan's team brought the two guards deeper into the

forest, far from any of the four-wheel-drive trails that linked the emergency exits around SNAKE. They were safely inside the collider ring, which was all it took to get the captured guards to talk.

The lead guard's name tape said Murphy. "I can't reveal our mission in full. You know that, right?"

Ethan appeared unsurprised. "For now, just tell me what I want to know."

Murphy leaned against a pine. "Our briefing was very clear about what to expect when we got here. They said there is a tunnel running in a hundred-mile circle under the foothills. Our CO came through here when we were setting up holding a topo map with the tunnel drawn on it. He pointed to the area I showed you and said we were not under any circumstances to pass through there, or we'd be in danger when the collider was turned off for good."

Phil looked at Ethan. "They are shutting this collider down, too?"

"They didn't tell me that," Murphy replied matter-of-factly.

"We turned off the power at CERN," Phil interjected. "I was there. We both were." He pointed at Ethan.

Murphy shrugged. "Above my pay grade. I heard some talk this morning that both of these magical rings were still making trouble. I guess it means one or both are still powered up."

"Fuck." Ethan rubbed his chin in deep thought. "I could take this detour if our mission was done, but it appears as if we failed."

"We don't know for sure," he suggested.

Murphy nodded. "I really have no idea about the other place. The only thing that matters is staying inside *this* ring. It's the only place on Earth they said is safe for us, so we have to protect it with our lives. They told us over and over."

Phil puzzled it out. "The ground below the SNAKE supercollider is going to protect you? Is that why you can't leave the boundary? Is SNAKE some kind of home base for when the power gets turned off?"

Murphy smiled. "Yes! That's a perfect way of describing it. Stay within the ring and live through the upcoming shitshow. Right on, uh, sir."

If they shut off the power and were shot across the planet, he wondered if turning it off on this end would send them back to CERN?

They needed more intel.

I-70, Kansas

Buck had to brush aside a wet mass of the dead locusts plastered to his hood so he could reach his windshield, which brought back some bad memories. "I spent some time burning shit with diesel back in the Sandbox. That was sick, but at least I didn't have to put my hands in it."

They'd pulled off the highway a hundred feet before the ramp to I-70.

Connie stood with Mac in front of the Peterbilt so the pup could do his business. She listened to him talk but stared vacantly to the west.

"You with me, lady?" he asked in a kind voice.

She turned and seemed to notice him. "Sorry. I was thinking about Phil. I swear he's out there." She pointed toward the sun, which was low in the sky.

After getting free of the locust storm, Buck had driven his truck as if it were a rental. They had made it out of Nebraska and halfway across Kansas in about two hours, and now the highway to Kansas City was within sight. Because they'd made such good time, he decided it was safe to get out and do a little KP.

He used his squeegee to scrub off the bugs caked on his windshield. The carcasses fell onto his hood, adding to the two inches of bodies already there. It turned his stomach because of the thick goo holding the bunch together like glue.

"I know he is. And *my* son is two hours that way." He pointed the squeegee to the east. "We've got one more city to go, then we'll head back west if that's where you think we'll find Phil."

"He could be in New Mexico," she suggested. It was also to the west.

Mac ran in circles, happy to be free. There was no time for the ball, and he was all out of meat-stick treats, so a run in the sun had to suffice.

After pushing another section of slop off his window, he turned to talk to her.

"We didn't meet by random chance, then go through this nightmare, only to find out your son didn't make it. Garth is going to survive all this, and so is your Phil. We only need the time to make it happen."

He didn't bring up the talk of nuclear war, time anomalies, or the insects stuck on crazy. Much like burning the latrine pits with diesel, it was best to hold your nose and power through it.

Buck looked back at Eve, Monsignor, and Sparky, who were working together to clean the rigs parked behind his. His team was prepared to go the distance, and he was happy that they only had two hours to go before he could prove to them it was all worth it. He embraced the role, too. Once he had his son, he was going to find them a place of safety. The radio continued to talk of cities designated as safe zones.

He wanted to go west to somewhere like Denver, his original destination, but it might be hard to pass up other cities if he could ensure his friends and his son would be safe there.

When the windshield was clear, he took a few minutes to run in circles with Big Mac. The exercise helped restore some of his energy. He wasn't going to say it, but he was beat.

No mistakes, Buck.

FIFTEEN

Columbia, MO

"Garth, look! They're pulling off the highway."

He'd been driving at almost a hundred miles an hour for the past ninety minutes. It was early evening, and the sun was a baking-hot orb low in the west. He'd been driving all day, and he and the car were now on fumes.

"Thank God," he replied, "I, uh, need to pee."

"Me too," she said with more excitement than him. The filthy travel restrooms they'd been using weren't up to any standard of cleanliness he supported, but Lydia was ecstatic to use toilets more substantial than a piece of wood with a hole in it.

"Let's do this. We only need a little more gas to get us to Kansas City. If we need more money after that, my dad will take care of it." He looked forward to letting his dad take over for him.

He pulled into the same gas station as the police caravan, although he had some fear there wouldn't be enough gas pumps. However, the modern travel station had more than enough for all of them.

As soon as he turned off the motor, he read the hand-printed signs taped nearby.

"Cash only. $20/gallon, all blends."

He pulled his small wad of bills out of the tiny pocket in his jeans.

Oh, shit.

A crumpled twenty and some ones were all he had left.

What would his dad do? It had been the guiding question of the trip. He was certain it was at least another hour or two to Kansas City. There was a little gas left in the tank, but adding one gallon wasn't going to help much.

Garth looked around and saw nothing but police cars. The uniformed men hustled to fill their tanks or run inside with the civilians riding with them. He figured they were the families of the officers.

"Hold on, Lydia. I've got to talk to them."

She stood next to the car, intending to watch over Garth as he pumped. It was the security system they had worked out. "Really? Won't they get you in trouble?"

It was risky, but without gas, his journey was going to end in a few more miles, no matter what.

"I don't think so. Not this time." He waved her along. "Come with me. You are less of a threat than me."

"I'm a fighter!" She gave the least-threatening punch he'd ever seen.

"I have no doubt, but I need you to look helpless. Can you do that?"

She slumped her shoulders and put on a sad face.

"Don't oversell it. Stand normally but don't say anything, okay?"

They walked together to the nearest police car. A large African-American policeman held the nozzle while filling up his cruiser.

"Excuse me, sir. We're going to Kansas City—"

"I saw you following us. You should slow down. We're moving too fast for you to be safe."

He laughed despite himself. "None of us are safe. I've been attacked by mobsters, and almost died in a New York Subway. I even attacked a dinosaur."

The officer furrowed his brow. "You on drugs?"

Garth reeled and tried to think of a response. "No. Hey, what happened to the Arch?"

"It's gone. Went away last night when the sky got all messed up."

"I came from the East Coast. It's as bad there. Please, my dad is in Kansas City. I just need a couple of gallons of gas to make it there."

"Looks like you stole a taxi. Is that what I'm seeing?" The officer didn't miss a thing.

"It's my dad's," he said lamely.

"And he's in Kansas City?"

Garth began to feel like he was in over his head, but the back door of the police cruiser opened. He noticed the woman for the first time.

"Jonesy, we can help these poor children, can't we?"

The officer seemed to suck in his slightly oversized gut. "That's my sister and her four kids." He sighed as he glanced at his sister. "Fine, Trish, I'll help them. Stay inside, okay?"

"Thank you, ma'am," Lydia said with a curtsey.

"You're just lovely, dear. I adore your dress and bonnet. You look like you belong in a one-room schoolhouse in the woods."

"I was!" Lydia beamed.

Jones came over and held out his hands like he was

going to shake with Garth. "Take this money, but don't let anyone see it. There are thieves everywhere. Get back in your car, and stay on the highway. We're heading west to Denver. If you get to your dad, you should go out there, because the police bands are filled with my law enforcement brothers and sisters doing everything they can to make it there before things get bad."

"*Before* they do? Um, Officer, you *do* realize—"

"Just take it," Jones insisted.

Garth clumsily shook hands and slid the money into his front pocket.

"Thank you, sir. You're a lifesaver."

The huge black man smiled. "It's nice to help someone again. I was beginning to think it was futile to even try since there's so much going wrong with the city of St. Louis. Remember, get to Denver."

Lydia half-turned to go but he held his ground. "Sir, we've heard of lots of cities with safe zones. Why aren't the police going somewhere closer? Denver is like five states away."

Jones looked him in the eyes as if appraising his soul. When he seemed satisfied, he leaned in to speak quietly. "You needed to pay more attention in geography class, son."

Garth did a double-take as the man continued, "I'm not sure anywhere is safe. We're heading to Denver because of a captain in the Missouri Highway Patrol. That's where he and his men are going, and they swear it's the only safe place in America. I guess we all follow the herd in one way or another."

"I'm following you guys," Garth blurted.

"Better hurry, kid, although it might be crowded in the men's room. Every car is filled to the brim with family and refugees we picked up on the trip here. Makes for some cramped quarters during the pit stops. We're speeding out of here the second everyone is done, so don't waste time."

"I have to pee!" Lydia said a little too loud.

Garth was embarrassed by her statement, but she only seemed concerned with getting inside.

"Good luck out there," the officer said as he walked back over to his pump.

"You too."

Garth had stuffed the rifle in the back seat on the floor under a blanket. He remembered that he should have been worried, but after the fact. He smiled at the foresight that he had forgotten.

He stumbled along next to Lydia as they headed for the store. He pulled out the two bills the officer had given him and confirmed he now had sixty dollars. In the new economy, it would get him three gallons of gas.

Would that be enough?

I-70, Kansas City

Buck's phone rang as he drove over the Kansas River at the western edge of Kansas City. The sun had gone down a half-hour prior, so there was only a bit of natural light left in the sky.

"Hot damn! It's Sam's parents."

"Garth's friend," Connie replied, confirming she remembered who they were from Buck's brief mention of them.

He picked up his phone. "Hello? Christian? Tell me you and Colleen are okay?"

"Buck! I can't believe we got through. Your phone hasn't rung in days."

138

"I've been driving. Right now, I'm in Missouri."

Christian spoke to someone on his end before returning to the call. "Colleen says hello. Sam does, too."

Buck was good friends with the family who'd kept an eye on Garth for most of the two years he'd been on the road. He felt bad that he hadn't made an effort to call them, but once Garth had said he wasn't evacuating with them, he'd put all his worry into his son. He wasn't going to second-guess that.

"I'm glad to hear from you. How are you guys making out with the radiation cloud and all that hubbub? Garth said it was mostly a bust."

"Oh, Garth got out? Sam has been worried sick about him. Me and Colleen couldn't believe he let Garth go out on his own, and I have to apologize that our son didn't think to keep a better eye on his friend."

He was glad Garth had split up with Sam, but he didn't want to use those exact words with the boy's parents.

"It's all water under the bridge. Garth drove a stolen taxi most of the way out here. He's with a young girl, apparently. We're going to meet him in a few miles, in fact."

Christian cleared his throat. "I can't tell you how happy that makes me. I've been worried sick we'd set Garth loose on the world and you'd be angry we let him go."

"Where are you?" he asked.

"Stamford, Connecticut. It's a FEMA evacuation point for New York City. First, it was for the nuclear fallout, but now it is for something they call disaster security."

"When can you go home?" Buck wanted to hear him say the trouble was ending.

"No word. New York is in the throes of a blackout, so it has been cordoned off. I mean, I'd understand if the radiation had come and made a mess of things, but that turned out to be fairly minor. A little escaped the Three Mile Island complex, and it made people sick in Philadelphia, but it didn't make it as far as New York City."

"You're anxious to go back home?"

Christian laughed. "Definitely. Don't let anyone tell you these FEMA beds are survivable, because they aren't. It's like sleeping on plywood sheets."

Kansas City was nearly devoid of vehicle headlights as they drove through downtown on the interstate. A few sharp turns and lane merges required some of his attention, but he'd been through there enough times to do it almost without thinking.

"Listen, Christian. Thank you for all you've done over the years, taking care of my boy. It really made a difference in our lives. I even socked away enough to send Garth to a state college. That's huge."

He had gone right into the Marines after high school, and right into a driver's seat after going back to permanent civilian status. College had never been on his radar, so helping his son do better than him had been a huge factor in the long days and weeks away from him.

"Oh, don't worry about it." His laughter seemed fatalistic. "You don't sound like you plan on coming home, Buck. Everything all right?"

"I'm fine. I can make plans all day long, like getting back to Staten Island, but that might not be possible." He looked at Connie. Someone back in her time was undoubtedly wondering when she would come back home. A lot of people were destined to be disappointed. "I might end up somewhere out here for a while, at least until life gets back to normal."

"FEMA is saying it won't be longer than a few more days. Then we can go back."

Buck didn't believe it, but it was little more than a feeling.

"Well, let's agree to get back to the island as soon as we can. Please give Colleen my best, and I can't wait to tell Garth that Sam is safe with you."

They'd crossed all of downtown Kansas City while he was on the phone. Now they were driving through old residential neighborhoods at the edge of the urban core.

"I'll tell Sam the good news, too. Glad to hear everyone is safe."

Once again, Buck didn't correct Christian's interpretation of their current dilemma. He wasn't in a FEMA camp enjoying "disaster security" like Sam's family, nor did he want to worry those guys about what it was like on the outside.

He smiled. "We'll talk soon. Good luck, Christian."

"Bye, Buck."

When he hung up, a convoy of police cars came around a corner on the westbound lanes of the interstate. They ran with their lights on and wove around slower vehicles like they were leading the Cannonball Run. The sirens wailed for only a few seconds before they sped out of earshot.

"Where's the fire?" Connie joked.

"No kidding. What do you think they're running from?"

She sat up. "Shit. I didn't think of that."

Connie took the phone from his hand. "Mind if I try Phil again?"

"Please do. I'll keep watch."

Buck was pleased that his front windshield was almost clear of the bug juice. He watched far up the road ahead, constantly expecting trouble to reveal itself.

"We both will." She held the phone to her ear but peered out front, same as him.

"We're almost at Blue Springs," he said dryly. "Just a few more miles."

SIXTEEN

***Search for Nuclear, Astrophysical, and Krono-
metric Extremes (SNAKE). Red Mesa, Colorado***

"Dr. Johnson, would it be all right if I went down to the auditorium with Missy so I could see for myself that everyone is in good health?"

He appeared shocked. "What do you think we would do to them? We're here to protect you."

Faith pointed to Bob. "You did notice one of your people 'protected' Dr. Stafford?"

"Serves him right," someone in the back of the room mumbled.

Dr. Johnson didn't seem interested in a debate. "Sure, go down there. Take him with you."

She thought it made logical sense, but Bob raised his hands. "Pass. I'm too dizzy to move, even if I do have to stay in this hostile work environment." He laughed and spat blood on the carpet in protest.

"That's sick," a nearby woman complained.

"I'll be back as soon as I can," she told Bob and the others.

She and Missy walked in silence until they got into the auditorium. At that point, the guard stood at the door with a couple of other soldiers, leaving the pair of them free from observation.

Faith spoke quietly. "You were right, Missy, I do want to warn the people at CERN. I need you to get the phone number of someone there. I don't care what kind of danger it puts us in, but we can't allow Dr. Johnson and his allies to nuke them off the map without having a chance to evacuate. That is barbaric."

The other woman thought about it. "Say I get a number; what are you going to use to call? We got our phones back after the NORAD troops came here, but this new group made us turn in every item they didn't like, including tablets, laptops, and phones. They were very thorough."

She looked around the giant underground auditorium. It was well-lit, so it was easy to see soldiers with guns up on the stage, in addition to those standing at each of the main exits.

Faith reassured her, "You do the best you can. Leave the hard part to me."

"That's why you get paid the big bucks, I guess."

She laughed a little. "Whatever we get paid, it isn't enough for what we've gone through." Faith suddenly turned miserable. "Missy, I was almost killed in one of those bomb blasts in the tunnel. I saw General Smith get blown to bits."

In her mind's eye, she saw the explosion again. It hadn't stopped playing in the background of her thoughts since it happened. Though she didn't exactly see the moment the general died, she had seen his remains after the fact. It had been more than enough.

Missy offered comfort by holding her hands. "I'm so sorry."

"I'll get over it. In fact, if I can pull this off, it will almost make up for his death. General Smith didn't give his life to help us survive while innocent people in Switzerland get killed. He wasn't that kind of man."

Missy smiled and nodded.

Faith tapped her on the shoulder. "Okay, let's get this done."

"Talk soon," Missy replied in a hushed voice.

That left Faith standing at the edge of the audience. A quick survey of faces nearby didn't reveal the person she was searching for, so she casually walked down the aisle next to the wall. When she made it to the front corner, she stopped and looked around some more.

Come on, be in here.

She feared outsiders might have been removed from the SNAKE facility completely. Dr. Johnson had mentioned something about quotas, and he celebrated the fact more scientists had been brought in, but he didn't say anything about kicking out the reporters.

Benny was nowhere in sight.

Faith walked in front of the stage and tried not to think about all the men with guns a few yards away.

"Dr. Sinclair!" Benny raised his hand to flag her down. He and his wife were about ten rows in, and a few seats away from the middle aisle.

She acknowledged him by walking his way. When she arrived at his row, she sat in an empty seat next to him.

"What brings you down here? Have something to report?" It was a joke, and meant as such, because Benny was in quarantine with the rest of them. "It might be a while before I can pass it along."

"I'm sorry I wasn't able to get you a scoop, Benny, but I had every intention of letting you in on what we'd found down in the ring. Did they tell you General Smith died saving us all?"

"They said something about that when we were rounded up, but they didn't give out any details."

Her heartbeat sped up as she moved closer to doing something sure to get on Dr. Johnson's bad side. She took a deep breath and gripped the arm of the chair to help her stay calm.

"Benny, what would you say if I had the story of the century? Maybe...ever."

"Pass," he said immediately. "I'm like Charlie Brown and the football, doctor. You've screwed me over since I came to SNAKE. Now, I'm thankful you got my wife in here, but we've done nothing but live under armed guards. I'm beginning to think I jumped the gun on all this. Maybe we should have gone to her mom's like she wanted."

"I know it's tough," she readily admitted, "but please understand none of that was by choice. General Smith was protective of his operation, and Dr. Johnson's people make Smith look like a teddy bear. This is literally the first time I've been able to talk to you about what's really happening in here."

Benny looked at his wife, then up to the stage, and finally back at her.

He whispered. "And what, pray tell, is that?"

She told him everything.

Australia

Dez stayed on the main deck of the *Majestic* for much of the morning. The ship departed the harbor without her jumping into the water, and Zandre left her alone once he was sure they were too far from land for her to bail.

She did not feel good about her decision.

I'm on my way, Faith.

She had tried calling her big sister, but the network didn't respond. She had no idea if it was because she was at sea or if the mobile phone network was still jiggered.

After pocketing her phone again, she walked the deck, noting how crates of supplies had been haphazardly stacked everywhere possible. Some of it was marked as food, some as dry goods. Russian letters were printed on one, along with the numbers 7.62x39. By all indications, her people in the Sydney Harbor Foundation had taken her warning to heart, and they had loaded everything they could carry on the boat.

What bothered her was that they had been willing to leave without her.

"No good deed goes unpunished," she mouthed.

Destiny stood near the bow when the front of the ship rose out of the water a couple of meters. The speed was cut in half as if they'd hit something or run aground.

"Fuck me!"

She tumbled against the railing.

The hard knock caused everything on the deck to shift too, like someone failing to whisk a tablecloth out from under the place settings.

Motion down in the water caught her eye, and it was apparent they'd run into a giant animal. Its gray back was similar to that of a crocodile, although no croc was big enough to be the mammoth thing below.

"What the hell are you?"

She ran along the side rail as the weight of the ship finally forced the monstrosity back under the water. It

147

didn't appear to move, and it stayed almost directly below her as she jogged toward the back.

The engines growled as if the captain had decided to hit the throttle after contact was made.

"It's a—" she shouted to anyone who could hear her. "It's a giant!"

The animal rolled forward as its body slid along the hull, a lot like a baker rolling dough under her palm. It allowed her to get a view of the animal in profile, but it was now about twenty feet under the water, so visibility was far worse.

Men and women ran out of the side compartments, intent on seeing what they'd struck.

The beast continued under the ship as she ran to the rearmost railing to watch it emerge.

"What was it, mate?" a man yelled as he arrived next to her.

There was some red blood swirling in the propeller churn behind them, but the animal wasn't to be seen. She hoped that meant it was only injured and was still able to swim away.

"I saw it, clear as day, but I don't have any clue what to tell you. It was big like a whale, tough like a croc, and vulnerable like a fish."

"And big as an island," the man added. "Do you know how big it had to be to lift our hull?"

"I guess we'll never know," she said dryly.

Destiny watched from the stern for a long time. Mainly to see if the creature would show itself again, but she also noted how far they were from mainland Australia. It was a sliver of gray on the horizon.

"So many new animals to catalog, and here I am running to save myself."

After pulling out her phone, she tried Faith again.

"Come on, sis. I really need to hear a friendly voice right now."

Kansas City, MO

"How many police cars do you think we've seen?" Connie pointed to another group of law enforcement vehicles speeding the opposite way on the highway.

"Too many to count. Hey, look. They have a fire engine!" The red safety vehicle seemed to have a dozen flashing lights. It went as fast as the cop cars.

"This is all kinds of fucked up, Connie. Where are they all going in such a rush?" It wouldn't surprise him to see police and fire during the end of the world, but they were all going the same direction on the same highway at the same rate of speed. It was as if a bulletin had been posted on a police-only website and these guys had heeded the call.

"I've never seen anything like it, even back in 2003."

The first thing that came to his mind was from the 1990 Gulf War. He had been a kid at the time, but he remembered the Highway of Death from the news broadcasts. He'd also seen films of it on the History Channel. Allied forces had caught Saddam's army while they retreated down a single highway in the desert. Aircraft tore them apart and left miles of wreckage in their wake.

"It's like a giant retreat," he said without getting into details. "They are all going to the same place, I guarantee it."

"Where is that, do you think?"

"No idea, but I'd be willing to bet they know something we don't."

He picked up the CB mic. "Break 9. This is Buck

Rogers. Any of you Smokies got your ears on?" He used generic trucker slang on the emergency channel, praying someone would pick up.

To his surprise, a man responded right away.

"Go ahead, break."

"Yeah, uh, I'm heading west on I-70. Mind if I hang out on your bumper?"

"Negative. You can follow us, though. We're going to...Wichita."

"Why the delay?" whispered Connie.

"Doesn't sound like you're too sure. Any chance you're going somewhere else?"

Buck had no fear of being caught. Even if the police wanted him, they would have no way of tracking him down while doing a hundred miles an hour. It was one of the advantages of using the citizen's band.

"Wichita. Over and out."

The line went silent for a few seconds, but then another male voice broke in.

"Bull. Shit." The signal was weak and filled with static, but it continued, "I've been tracking these assholes since Centralia, Illinois."

Buck wanted to talk to the new person, but his signal faded fast.

"Come again? What's your twenty?"

No reply, so he let it go.

If he had to guess, it was someone driving west along with the police. There were a few civilian cars, and sometimes even one or two big rigs trying to keep up with each group of law dogs.

Buck faced east, chasing his own target.

Garth was close. He felt it.

SEVENTEEN

I-70, Missouri

"And that was the last time the McCurry boys tried to pick up a snake, I'll tell you!"

Lydia had been doing her best to keep him awake, but the setting sun, long day, and stressful driving ganged up on him constantly. His eyelids drooped closed and popped open with disturbing regularity, no matter how hard he listened to her interesting tales of life in her time.

"It sounds great," he answered.

"No, haven't you been paying attention? It was terrible. Both brothers got bit that summer because they loved trying to scare us girls."

"Oh, right," he replied in a dreamy tone.

The headlights of traffic in the far lanes reminded him of fireflies dancing in the dusk. It was almost nine o'clock at night, and nothing was left of the sun but a warm smudge on the horizon. It was another tip-off for his tired mind to call it quits.

"How does my dad drive all day every day? I think I would die if I had to drive this much all the time." Garth happened to look down at the speedometer. "Oh, shit! I'm doing a hundred and ten!"

"It does feel as fast as lightning, Garth."

They had lost the police escort before they left Columbia, Missouri. Since he was late getting to the fuel pumps, everyone was done by the time he got started. He watched helplessly as the police caravan peeled out of the station and got right back on the interstate. A couple other civilian cars were late following too, but he had been dead last. By the time he finally got on I-70 to give chase, they were long gone.

He'd been driving dangerously over the limit for the past ninety minutes to try to catch them.

"I think this is the one time Dad would actually get out his belt and smack me with it. No joking this time. I'm going way faster than he would approve."

The taxi blasted by a much slower car doing the speed limit on his right side. It was almost routine for Garth, after doing it for a few hours, but deep in his last functioning brain cell, he acknowledged that one mistake might result in a crash that would kill all involved in an instant. That was what would anger his dad the most: he was taking too many risks.

"I wonder if Sam ever drove this fast? His parents would kill him if they ever found out he went over a hundred." He glanced down at the speedometer again. The number looked even more impressive in kilometers. "We're going almost 180 kilometers per hour."

"Is that different than miles per hour?" Lydia asked over the wind noise.

Garth had a hard time remembering. "We learned about it in school, I think. There's a conversion..." He tried to remember the formula, but he had a hard time concentrating on it. Something about a mile being one-point-something kilometers long.

"Garth!"

He jerked his head up. It surprised him to see a steering wheel in his hands.

"You were asleep!" Lydia shook him from side to side.

The rocking action was soothing.

"Garth!" she shouted again.

"What?" he replied with a touch of anger. "I'm fine."

She pinched the soft part of his upper arm.

"Ouch! What was that for?"

Lydia did it again even harder.

He recoiled from the pain. "Damn! Why?"

"Garth, you aren't acting normal. You were talking to yourself and adding numbers out loud. You've been pointing to the dial on the front there, and you get surprised every time you see it.

He looked where she pointed. The speedometer was now most of the way around the dial, and it pointed to the number 120.

"Da-amn!" he blurted.

"Slow down!" she shrieked.

It hurt his feelings to anger his pretty pioneer passenger, so he took her counsel seriously.

"I'm slowing down."

The motor had been throbbing as it struggled to deliver the needed horsepower to go as fast as a sports car, but it wasn't designed to do it for hours. When he let off the gas, the engine sounded angry.

"That's not good."

He hadn't given the car an ounce of care on their journey. He absently wondered if the taxi was overdue for service, and he was now paying for the delay. Or maybe

Dawson the car thief had taken it from a taxi service depot, and it had already been broken. Or maybe—

"Garth!" Lydia grabbed the wheel this time. "You can't let go!"

He blinked about twenty times to make his mind comprehend what he saw ahead. There were the lights of a city, and a giant pair of golden arches hanging in the sky on the left side of the highway. With great effort, he pawed the wheel again.

"I can make it," he strained to say. If it were anyone else in the world, he would have willingly given up driving so his partner could take over. However, three days ago, Lydia had never seen a car, much less driven one.

On the other hand, Lydia had watched him drive nonstop for a whole day. Maybe she had picked it up? Would it be safer to let her try?

As he got closer to the truck stop, he was drawn to the bright glow of cheeseburger heaven like a moth to the light. He wasn't sure if he made it to the exit, but he figured he was close enough to get off the highway…

"Garth!"

Blue Springs, MO

Buck experienced a profound sense of dread after listening to the police lie to him on the CB radio. They weren't going to Wichita any more than he was going to White Plains. As more groups of police streamed by the parking lot of the McTruckStop, he knew they were the key to his family's survival.

"When Garth gets here, we're going after those guys. We're going to wear those police cars like pants and be on them so tight they can't kick us off."

He and Connie stood together on the wide parking lot of the mega-sized fast food restaurant and truck stop. She put her hand on his back as she leaned against his side. "You know I'll go wherever you go, but this seems like a long shot. We've only seen these police cars since we got on I-70. Why didn't we see them on I-80?"

"Maybe I-80 doesn't go where they need to go? What if, instead of driving west on I-80, the police up there decided to go south into Kansas." He was talking himself into believing they really were going to Wichita, but that still didn't feel right. They'd gone south from Nebraska too and seen a billion bugs, but not one police car.

"Well, all I know is we can't stay here." He pointed to the hamburger sign high in the sky. "And failing a miracle where we are instructed exactly where and when to go somewhere, I'm inclined to stick with what we know: go back out to Denver."

She studied him seriously for a couple of seconds, then relaxed. "I'm fine with going to Denver. It will keep me closer to home, for sure."

"I guess we're committed, Buck." Sparky and Eve had snuck up on them.

He turned around to face them. "You are going out west with us?"

Sparky shrugged. "I could have peeled off at any time. Eve could have done the same. I think we both want to see you find your son and then go wherever you think we'll be safe."

Buck suddenly felt the press of leadership. One wrong decision...

"I'm glad to have you with us. Do you know if Monsignor has made up his mind?"

Eve flipped her hair as she looked back at the other

driver. His hood was open, and Buck figured he was cleaning out bug carcasses. "Not yet. I think he wants to go with us, but we are relatively close to his drop. I think he can taste it."

Buck chuckled. "A week ago, I would have done anything to get this trailer to the depot. Today, I'd drop it and my semi if I believed it would save my family. Funny how the end of the world gives you a new perspective on the people in your life."

Eve absently swatted a big flying bug out of her face before freezing in place. "Uh-oh."

They all looked into the darkness to see if a swarm of locusts might be upon them, but when nothing else attacked, Eve sighed. "I guess it was a loner."

"Maybe it came back to life from among the millions stuck to our trucks," Buck suggested. Their rigs were still caked with insects like someone had draped big, ugly blankets over their hoods and front bumpers. If he ever found an industrial truck wash and had the luxury of some time, he was going to spring for the most expensive cleaning package to get all those bugs off his beloved Peterbilt.

Connie laughed. "Zombie bugs. That's all we need."

"Well," Sparky began, "they still aren't saying shit about the nuke hits down in the Southwest, but at least they haven't reported any other cities getting blown up."

"You noticed that, too?" Buck shot back. "We've been listening for news all day, and it seems like the more miles we put on, the less they say about what's happening in America and elsewhere."

"And the news is all the same, no matter which channel." Eve brushed her legs as if to shove off any bugs. "They talk about the bombs going off, then list a bunch of cities where the government has set up help centers."

"The news hasn't told me one useful thing since all this started," Buck stated. "I've learned the most from truckers on the CB, other drivers I met in person, and my own eyes. Now we hear police lying to our faces when we ask them where they're going. Hell, it's just like it's always been. We can only really depend on ourselves."

"We still going to that SNAKE place?" Sparky glanced at Eve before looking directly at Buck. "Yesterday, you said the convoy of military gear was heading there. Maybe these police units are going there too?"

Denver was hundreds of miles away. It was highly unlikely all these police and fire units had gotten the same memo to pass by other cities designated as safe zones so they could go to one far away.

None of his past experiences suggested law enforcement would pass people in need to go somewhere safe themselves. They were usually the guys running into danger, not unlike him and his fellow Marines.

What am I missing?

"I guess the honest answer is that I'm not sure what we're going to do. Let me get my son first, then we'll all decide as a group where we're going to go. That will be a good time for Monsignor to make his decision, although I'll tell you right now that I'm going to petition him hard to stick with us."

He hadn't heard from Garth since his son was in Louisville, so it was hard to know how long he'd have to wait for him to arrive. He held his phone in his left hand so he wouldn't miss a call if Garth tried to dial him again with a stranger's phone, but it had been silent since Christian called.

Buck made a fist with his free hand, then released it. Once his hand was open, he did it again out of habit.

Connie gripped his fingers after he'd done that about ten times.

"Thanks. I guess I'm getting nervous."

"I know the feeling," she assured him. "I'm finally going to get to meet the fine young man you've been raising."

EIGHTEEN

***Search for Nuclear, Astrophysical, and Krono-
metric Extremes (SNAKE). Red Mesa, Colorado***

"This is incredible." Benny's voice was subdued as he finally replied to Faith after she explained some of what had taken place. "The four links are necessary to keep the experiment running, but someone from the outside came in and tried to destroy them? Were we that close to the apocalypse?"

She kept her voice low, too. "I'm not sure what would have happened. The new group is upstairs. They showed us a film laying it all out. Dr. Johnson was teleported here—"

Benny held up his hand. "Wait a second. Are you screwing with me? This isn't very funny."

"I'm a scientist, Benny. When it comes to my work, I have a sense of humor measured in Planck lengths. I would never lie to you. We're way beyond that."

"Plank what?"

"It's a small unit of measurement. Beyond microscopic."

"Okay, I get it."

She did her best to explain the film and the theory of how Dr. Johnson might have been sucked from CERN and deposited in SNAKE. She finished by telling him of Johnson's warning.

"The takeaway is SNAKE survives, and CERN is destroyed? I can live with that." He sat back in his chair like the story had resolved itself to his satisfaction.

Missy caught her attention at the far end of the row, so she waved her to come to the middle aisle.

"Benny, this is very important. I need you to get me in touch with the outside. I have to warn the people at CERN to get clear, and you need to warn the rest of the world."

"What are you saying?"

She leaned in close. "My assistant is getting me the number for someone at CERN. I have to find a phone and contact them. I only need a minute to tell them to get out. Then, you tell your newspaper to broadcast our location to citizens everywhere. They've got to come inside the ring of our supercollider."

"Where they'll be safe," he said dryly.

"Yes. That's what I've suspected for the past couple of days, but Dr. Johnson confirmed it. It's the reason why he brought his people here. They aren't here only to end the experiment. They're here to survive it."

She glanced at Missy, who was close.

"Benny, I told you at the start you could make a difference. I'm depending on your reporter's tenacity to figure out how to make this happen."

Missy bent over and handed her a piece of paper. "I found someone in the IT group, Faith. He knew the number to CERN by heart because he has to call it every day to coordinate with the tech people there."

"Brilliant." Faith beamed. "Thank you."

Missy stood up and walked away.

The quick meeting caught Benny's attention. "You two are pulling something, aren't you?"

Faith nodded. "She was one part of my plan. Can you get me in touch with the outside?"

Benny turned to face his wife, who sat on his other side. Faith was unable to hear what he said, but his wife quietly said yes.

"As a matter of fact, I have access to a phone right here and now."

Her mouth dropped open. "How?"

Benny looked around. "I told you they didn't check my wife when she came in. They also didn't pat her down well enough when we were rounded up again." He chuckled. "They should have used TSA screeners. Those assholes wouldn't hesitate to pat down Jesus coming through in a wheelchair. The soldier kid who checked out my wife seemed embarrassed to touch her. It worked out for the best."

"She has it right now?" Faith asked skeptically. It was too perfect.

"Yes, but obviously we can't use it in here."

They both sat back in their seats as if a movie was about to start. She ran through some ideas on how she could get the phone and then go somewhere private to use it. However, the only place where she might be left alone was the restroom, and she couldn't talk on the phone and not be overheard there.

Hundreds of scientists and technicians sat around her, chit chatting to keep themselves occupied. If she weren't saddled with the role of their leader, she could easily settle in and relax with the people she had once worked with.

The guards remained at the doors. They also talked

with each other in a relaxed fashion. She figured it was because there was nowhere for the captive audience to go. Guards manned the doors. They patrolled the hallways. They were at the emergency exits of the base.

"We have to do it here," she said out of the side of her mouth.

"What?" he blurted. "Are you nuts?"

"We may never get the perfect opportunity. There are too many people talking right now to overhear any one conversation. As long as I keep my head down like I'm thinking, or sick, I can at least get a quick message to CERN. You have to let me try."

Benny mulled it over for a minute, but he leaned forward in the manner she described. "If you sit like this, I think it will work."

"I'll call my people first, then you call yours. Deal?"

"Wait a second," he replied. It took him a few minutes, but she watched as he and his wife worked together to get the phone to him. First, she took it out of her shirt, then, she gave Benny a hug. At some point, they made the switch, and he had it ready to pass to her.

Please don't let it get quiet.

People continued to talk all around her, so she got out the piece of paper and dialed the number.

The phone didn't even ring once. A man picked up. "Hello. This is the European Organization for Nuclear Research, operations department. Who is this?"

"CERN? In Switzerland?" She had to be sure.

"Yes. This is the IT support line, but no one is here right now to answer your call. It is the middle of the night. Can you call back tomorrow?"

"No! It's an emergency. This is going to be hard to believe, but I know for a fact that the United States government is planning to destroy your facility using a nuclear bomb. They want to destroy you because of the experiment you're running."

"Experiment? Which one? We have several going on." The man sounded worried.

"It wasn't on your official list of projects. It was...done illegally."

She didn't want to get into the weeds of how Azurasia Heavy Industries worked with secretive government groups to set up and run the experiment without full consent from either supercollider.

Someone tapped Faith on the shoulder. When she looked up, the woman stood in the aisle next to her. "Hey, I see you have a phone. Can I use it?"

Faith was shocked beyond words because the woman made no effort to be secretive.

Idiot!

She held a "wait" finger to the woman, then talked into the phone.

"I have to go," she said as fast as possible to the CERN employee. "I'll call you back as soon as I can. You have got to make sure people stay away from your location. Get everyone out of Geneva if you can!"

The man laughed. "Based on a random call in the middle of the night? No one would believe me."

She was in danger of failing.

"I'll call you back. Who is this, by the way? I'm Doctor Faith Sinclair. I work at SNAKE in Colorado."

"Oh, right. I know of you. I'm Doctor Kyle Johnson."

She hung up the phone, then looked at the clueless woman.

"There appears to be two Doctor Kyle Johnsons. I'll

play along until one of them comes clean that she's the imposter."

Red Mesa, CO

Ethan's Task Force Blue 7 was almost back up to full staff. During the afternoon, Phil and the Air Force airmen managed to track down a couple more of the original enlisted men who had been in Switzerland with him. The only two missing were the driver and navigator from the Fox.

"Do you have the map drawn?" Ethan asked Phil.

"Yes." He'd drawn it on a small square of scratch paper. "We now know where the ring is located below us, at least around here. Obviously, it goes in a loop for sixty-two miles so we can't map it all out, but we know it goes out toward the flat ground below the foothills." He pointed through the stand of pines toward the Dakota Hogback, which was barely visible through the thick trees.

Ethan leaned against a trunk in the shadowy grove they'd made their command post. "Good work, Phil. We can use this to keep our area of operations near the border of the collider."

Phil stood closer so the prisoners wouldn't hear. "You believe what he said about disappearing?"

Ethan shrugged. "It doesn't matter. If he and all these other guards believe they'll be erased if they go outside this ring, it gives us a powerful advantage over them. We can move outside at will. Avoid capture."

He couldn't find fault with the suggestion, although he privately harbored some misgivings about going outside the ring and being left behind. As fantastic as it sounded, he couldn't write it off.

Ethan continued. "Have you made any progress on figuring out his unit's composition? Strength? Weapons?"

"Not really. The 130th isn't a real division in the US order of battle. I believe it was a fake unit from back in World War II."

"Yes. I couldn't place it until you said it." Ethan looked around. "Was the unit reactivated as some kind of decoy, or is it now a legitimate division like he said? If it's up to fighting strength, does that mean ten thousand men and women came along with him?"

"Grafton and I were able to reconnoiter this afternoon. We got closer to the parking area they've set up. Our best guess is there are five hundred new vehicles out there. Figure at least two thousand civilians. Humvees and other heavy equipment are parked up the hill under cover, so it's harder to estimate force size."

"Sounds like they brought their families."

"Agreed," Phil replied. "Murphy said as much. Not only does he not want us to put him outside the boundary line, but he also doesn't want his family put in danger either."

"Who could blame him? Go on."

"Sir, this is more of a heavy mechanized division. We saw bulldozers constantly working on tank emplacements like they're expecting the Soviets to speed across Kansas and attack. We guess maybe fifty tanks, two hundred light vehicles, and we think we heard Paladins driving in the woods. At least platoon strength. We even saw a lone Buffalo parked in front of the main offices of SNAKE like it was a trophy."

"Damn. We're lucky they haven't found us."

Phil gave him a casual salute. "Good leadership has kept us in the fight."

"Yeah, but who are we fighting? A mystery division dug in on home soil. We haven't heard shit from anyone up the chain, and all we know is we're on the wrong damned continent. There is no chance of finishing our mission if we're sitting out here pissing in the pines."

"Sir, Murphy was very clear that his basic orders were to keep civilians from interfering with this place. Does that sound like official military doctrine to you? Shouldn't we be helping people come here if this is really a safe place?"

"'Safe place?' That's not our mission, Phil, and you know it."

"Rangers lead the way, sir. I'll follow your orders until our assignment is done. I'm simply not sure I agree with the mission of these other guys." He jerked a thumb over his shoulder at the prisoners.

"No. Something isn't right about them. Keep at it, Phil. We've got to have more intel before we can decide what to do, next."

Blue Springs, MO

Buck didn't want to let go of Connie's hand, but it looked like they were going to be on the parking lot for a while, so he wanted to take Big Mac out for a walk. However, the instant he let go, a metallic buzzing sound caught his attention on the highway. A westbound car had run into the grassy median.

His stomach went into his throat as he listened to the car get tangled in the retention cable.

"Fuck! That's Garth." Without thinking, he ran toward the accident.

"How do you know?" Connie cried, chasing him.

It was the fastest hundred-yard dash he'd done since

high school. He strained to see the crashed vehicle as he ran, but it was hard to see anything in the darkness. The cable stopped the car from crossing the median and driving into the McTruckStop on this side of the highway, but it was impossible to know if the driver was all right.

He quickly established it was a black car, which matched what Garth had said he was driving.

You don't know it's him.

As he sprinted over the empty eastbound lanes, he realized he was being stupid. His first instinct could have been wrong, and he might be running to the rescue of some random stranger while putting himself in danger.

As crazy as he felt, he didn't slow down.

He sprinted into the grassy median, intent on helping. When he got a few yards from the car, he noted that the black paint job was a mess. The accident had scraped off a wide band of paint, exposing the original yellow.

Garth had been proud he'd painted the taxi.

The airbags had gone off, blocking his view of the survivors in the front seats, but he bashed the nearest one to help get it out of the way.

Be okay, whoever you are.

After a slight delay, he saw messy hair he'd recognize anywhere.

He was ready to puke from nervousness because he still couldn't see his condition.

"Garth! Are you okay, son?"

The airbags finally deflated, revealing a pair of kids. The girl in the passenger seat was dressed like she'd fallen through a crack in time from the Civil War era. She perfectly matched the girl Garth said he was traveling with.

And the boy...

Garth's face looked normal.

No blood.

He's awake!

"Garth!" he repeated, desperate to hear he was fine.

"Oh, hey, Dad. Don't worry, we've been sleeping in separate beds the whole time."

Buck laughed like he'd been saving it up for a month.

NINETEEN

Blue Springs, MO

"You made it, son. You're safe."

Garth looked up at him. "Where am I?"

After the wreck, Buck had helped Garth walk over to the parking lot for the McTruckStop. He'd made him sit down at the base of the tall pole supporting the twin arches. Connie had brought Lydia and sat her next to Garth.

"You're at the truck stop where I asked you to meet me." He got choked up. "I don't know how you did it, but you drove halfway across the country in twenty-four hours."

Lydia sat up. "He drove us faster than any speed I ever could have imagined. It was a hundred and twenty before he fell asleep for good."

"One-twenty?" Buck bellowed. "What were you, fuh-freaking insane?"

Connie touched his shoulder, which immediately calmed him, but he breathed in and out a few times to step away from the cliff.

Garth acted like he didn't know his father was mad. "Don't get the belt, Dad. I was in good company. Some police cars let me travel with them. I only went that fast because they did."

He rubbed his chin and finally laughed. "Yeah, I guess you're getting too old for the belt." More seriously, he went on, "We've seen a lot of those cops driving by. This is really important, Garth. Do you know where they're going?"

"Yes," Garth replied. "I talked to an officer a couple of hours ago. He was from St. Louis and said he and all his pals were going to Denver. Isn't that where you've been telling me not to go?"

It's always Denver.

"I thought I was reading things right by telling you not to go there, but maybe I'm not right about everything."

Connie chuckled.

"What I mean is, we've got to pick somewhere to go where we'll all be safe. I don't think such a place exists, but people on the radio keep telling us of safe cities."

Garth's head bobbed like he was keeping himself awake only with a huge effort. "Dad, I tried to do what you would do, but I didn't pick up anyone but Lydia."

"That's good," he replied. "You picked up one person, and I think it was the perfect number." Buck glanced at Lydia. "I'm Garth's dad. You can call me Buck."

Lydia perked up. "He's talked about you a lot. I'm pleased to meet you."

"I have a million questions for you." He'd been wondering about Lydia's origins ever since Garth mentioned her on the ferry. How long ago was that? It felt like months, although it had only been two days. "First, however, I need to know if you are sore or need anything after your crash."

"I feel fine, but I'm disappointed in myself for letting this happen. Garth asked me to keep him awake as it became night, but once the sun went down, it was more difficult to think of things to say."

"We couldn't stop. Danger was everywhere. Couldn't let Lydia take over." Garth's upper eyelids seemed magnetically attracted to the lowers.

Lydia didn't take offense. "I cannot drive."

Buck chuckled. "Somehow, I bet you'd be a good driver. You hung with my son when he needed help, and I appreciate that more than you know."

Lydia grinned. "Garth said you would help me find my wagon train, but after living in your time, I don't think I ever want to go back. There are so many wonderful things in your world. I could live here forever."

Buck imagined he was talking to Connie. She hadn't expressed much excitement about the prospect of going back either. She wanted to find out if her son had survived Iraq, but she was happy in the year 2020. Despite the fact that with all their technological advances, none of his web searches had turned up anything on a Phil Stanwick. She didn't know that he had tried. He didn't want her to get her hopes up only to crush them moments later.

The time had come to make a decision about everyone's future.

Monsignor volunteered to drive Garth's taxi out of the median and park it next to Buck's Peterbilt. Looking at it from across the lot, the front wheel leaned outward at a strange angle. Buck was sure it was no longer safe to drive.

"Come on, guys. Let's get up and go back to the truck. We'll grab stuff out of your car, then you can ride with me."

"The weapon," Garth said carefully. "I have a rifle on the floor of the backseat, Dad. I'm sorry, too. I lost most of the guns I brought with me from the house. One of them got stolen by the mobster who talked to you on my phone."

Buck's blood pressure spiked just thinking about the mob guy. He still wished he could go back east, find the bastard, and go full Marine on him. However, he didn't want Garth to think he was upset about the firearms.

"He also left some of them behind when he saved my life from radiation."

That's my boy.

He beamed with pride as he walked his son up the parking lot and back to his truck. A second before he got to the bug-encrusted semi, he remembered the last call he'd taken.

"Sam is safe, son. I heard from his parents tonight."

Garth's eyes were practically shut as he climbed up into the sleeper. He didn't even seem to notice the caked-on locust mess. "No, they're not. None of us are safe. The lights are going to take Lydia away from me, and the rest of us are going to disappear like the St. Louis Arch. It's going to be bad..."

He shared a look of concern with Connie as she helped Lydia up the steps.

I have to prove him wrong.

Kansas City, KS

Garth had never felt safer. He snuggled into the warm sheets of his dad's truck, as he'd done on other overnight trips they'd taken together. He vaguely remembered a horribly long drive and a wreck he had barely survived, but it faded away before he let himself recall the details.

He rolled over, intending to sprawl out and revel in comfort, but something wet slapped against his face.

"What the hell?"

The lights inside the cabin were low because they were

on the road, but it was bright enough to see the panting Golden Retriever. The dog licked him again for good measure.

He recoiled in shock for a moment, but when he roused a bit more, he couldn't help but chuckle. "Aren't you a good pup?" Garth scratched the dog behind the ears. "Yes, you are."

A shape moved behind the dog.

A girl.

Lydia was under the same blankets as him, although she was still asleep.

He panicked, forgetting where he was for a second, before realizing he was in bed with a girl and a strange dog. Before he could straighten himself out, a redheaded woman crouched at the edge of the bed.

"I'm Connie," the woman whispered. "We met back at the McDonald's, but you were kind of sleepy."

"Hello, Connie. I'm Garth."

"I know. I've been traveling with your father for a few days now. The only thing that kept him going was knowing he would see you again. I think he's high on driving right now because he's so happy to have finally made it to you."

"I crashed," he said, suddenly remembering more.

"Don't worry about that. You're safe now. Buck is working on getting us somewhere where we can all be safe for good."

"The cops said they were going to Denver." He blurted it out as if it were important to impart the information.

Buck half-turned to him. "Thanks, son. That's where we're heading."

Garth replied with a thumbs-up.

"Tell him about his new friend," Buck said to Connie.

"Right. So, this is..." Connie whispered. "Big Mac." She

rubbed the Golden's back and spoke a little louder. "He loves to bark when he hears his name. I didn't want him to wake up your girlfriend."

"Oh, she's not my—"

"It's fine. I only meant she's a friend."

He thought he saw the woman wink at him, but he wasn't all the way with it, so he didn't comment on it.

"I love Golden Retrievers," he said quietly.

"Your dad got him for you. He explained how he picked up this pup when he left New York, and they've been traveling together for the past week. They were inseparable when he rescued me, so you might have to fight him for possession."

"Hey, now," Buck complained.

"My dad rescued you?"

She nodded. "I'll tell you all about it sometime. For now, get your rest, okay?"

It felt nice to have a motherly figure more or less tuck him in. It had been years since his own mother had done that. The sensation of safety led him deeper into the grasp of sleepiness. The rocking action of the truck in motion also helped.

"I'm glad I got to meet you, Garth." She got super-quiet again and spoke like she was from the South. "I knew you'd be a hero just like your daddy."

The flattery wasn't a requirement to fall asleep, but it added to the pile of things dragging him into Dreamland.

I'm never getting out of bed again.

He rolled away from Connie and Big Mac, intent on going right back to sleep. However, when he opened his eyes one last time, he saw the biggest grasshopper of his life crawling up the back wall of the sleeper.

"Bug!" he whisper-yelled.

All at once, he remembered seeing about a million locusts all over the side and top of his dad's truck as he got inside. Black streaks ran sideways on the door, as if the wind had blown the juicy insides toward the rear.

Connie chuckled. "You get used to them."

TWENTY

Search for Nuclear, Astrophysical, and Krono-metric Extremes (SNAKE). Red Mesa, Colorado

Faith had to pull rank on the woman who'd spotted her using a phone. It was a scientist she didn't recognize, which meant she was part of General Smith's contingent.

"I'm Dr. Sinclair, nice to meet you. Please, this phone call is a matter of worldwide importance, all right? I need you to walk away and pretend you didn't see this phone. If the guards see, they'll take it away."

"Can I use it later?"

Faith experienced a pang of guilt in advance of the lie she needed to tell. "Yes, when this is all over, you can use this phone as much as you want. The guards won't stop you, most likely."

"I'll be back," the woman casually replied.

Faith's heartbeat had been out of control since the woman almost gave her away. She scanned the edges of the room to see if any of the guards had noticed the interaction, but they were all busy talking to each other.

"Phew!" she let out.

"You getting anywhere?" Benny asked.

She re-dialed CERN. "Yes. I should be done momentarily."

Dr. Johnson picked up again. "This is CERN. Is this Dr. Sinclair?"

She hunched over in her seat as if she were extremely interested in her shoes. It allowed her to maintain a low-key conversation without raising her voice above the background noise of everyone else in the auditorium.

"Doctor Johnson, this is very important. You have to evacuate. They said they were going to send the military to get you out, but I guess they never arrived."

"They were here, yes. A group of American soldiers came into the facility earlier today, but Dr. Eli wouldn't say where they went. He left early, saying he had the mother of all headaches."

"They were there to evacuate you," she said in a calm, cool, and composed voice.

He chuckled. "If I called you in the middle of the night and said you had to abandon your facility, do you think you would do it? Oh, and if I also said you needed to evacuate Denver, do you think you could convince anyone to believe you? I'll save you the trouble: no, you wouldn't. You're welcome."

"Doctor, this isn't a joke." There was no way to prove she was telling the truth. "However, I see your point."

"Good," he replied.

"Listen, aren't you seeing any odd things going on there? Planes dropping from the sky? Disappearing landmarks? Weird weather?"

He laughed pleasantly. "We haven't had a good rain in a

month. We could do with some odd weather, I'll tell you that right now. As for weirdness, the only thing even remotely out of the ordinary was those military men showing up, then going missing, but they were with the Army, you know? They can do whatever they want without telling anyone about it. I'm sure they're out in the mountains somewhere having a good laugh at Dr. Eli's expense."

Faith schemed in her mind as she tried to think who she could call so they, in turn, would call CERN and confirm her story. General Smith had never told her who ran the show in Europe, so there were no ins there. The NORAD guards were no longer around so she couldn't ask them, either. There were no other options.

"Look, Dr. Sinclair, I know your voice from some videos you did during the construction of SNAKE, so I know you are who you say you are. You don't have the authority to shut down CERN, and this may surprise you to know, but I don't either. It has to go through the twenty-two-member council. If you give me a little more to go on, I might be able to present the idea to them as soon as they reconvene next month. Assuming that won't be too late?"

She didn't have a firm timetable, but the Dr. Johnson here at SNAKE had made it seem like the destruction was going to happen sooner rather than later.

"That's it!" Faith said a little too loud.

"What is?" the man on the phone replied.

"Doctor, I'll call you back. I'm going to talk to someone who's going to take care of you, okay?"

"This is one of the strangest phone calls I've ever had, but I'm working all night so I won't be going anywhere. I'd love to hear from someone who can confirm your fanciful plea."

"Talk soon." She hung up on him.

She was going to give the phone back to Benny because she wanted him to make the call to his boss before she risked losing the phone, but she had another person to call first.

Without shifting positions, she silently dialed the next number.

Off the coast of Australia

After striking the giant marine animal, the *Majestic* took about fifteen minutes to lower its scientific equipment into the water to see if they could find it again. However, no one wanted to delay for too long, and they were soon going full speed again.

Zandre leaned against the railing while he smoked a cigar in the afternoon sunshine. "You almost discovered another new species, Dez. I think this change, whatever you call it, is going to rewrite the animal kingdom in ways we can't anticipate. You play your cards right, and you'll make millions, mate."

"Me? Why me?" She was a naturalist, which was not exactly a high-paying field.

He flicked his cigar before glancing at her. "Imagine a zoo filled with all these wonderful new animals. Humanity is hungry for something different—a new experience. These extinct creatures could deliver that for decades to come."

"You sound like that bloke in *Jurassic Park*."

"Spared no expense," he said, mimicking the rich character who had set up the doomed park in the movie. "But seriously, I have the land, and you have the talent."

"Oi. This is about money?" Zandre had gone off to kill a Duck of Doom so he could collect a huge bounty. Sure, it was to pay off his property, but it was still a bit selfish to her way of thinking.

"No, this is about survival. We need to understand the animals dropping into our new ecosystem. I've lived my life as a hunter and guide in the bush, but I'd be happy to track and hunt animals so you could tranq them. Bring them back to our land. Understand what makes them tick."

She had to admit, it sounded better than what he did now.

The phone rang in her pocket.

"Holy shit! It's Faith!" She answered immediately.

"Hello? Dez? It's me." Her sister's voice sounded like it was coming from the other end of a long tunnel.

"I hear you!" she replied. "It's good to hear your voice."

"I can't talk for long," Faith spoke in an even tone, like she was calling from a library. "Where are you? Can you get to America?"

"I'm trying," she answered. "I'm on a boat heading there at this very minute. I convinced the Sydney Harbor Foundation they needed to go there, like you said."

"That's great," Faith replied with more emotion. "Where are you now?"

She looked around. Mainland 'Straya was out of view, but they were still at the start of their journey.

"Zandre, do you know how long it will take us to get to America?"

"The captain said it's going to take three weeks, assuming we don't run over any other monsters." He laughed and took another drag on his cigar.

"Crap, sis. It's going to take three weeks."

Far down the tunnel, Faith gasped.

"Will we make it in time?" Destiny asked her sister.

After a long pause, Faith replied. "I have no idea. Just keep coming, okay? Don't stop for anything, you hear me?"

"Yes, ma'am," she assured her. "I'll tell the captain to give me his best speed the whole way."

"Dez, I'm scared. The Army is going to nuke the collider in Europe, and people are going to die there. We don't know what it's going to do, but they say it will return things to normal here—just here, inside the ring."

That caught her by surprise. "So, I guess we're going to live with these strange animals all over the place. Zandre and I were talking about starting a zoo together. We're going to fill it with totally new species."

"You do that, sis, but only when you get back. I need you to promise you won't stop trying to get here, no matter what." Her voice echoed in a weird way, as if someone was messing with the sound tube between them.

"Three weeks will go by before you know it."

Faith was silent for a few moments, then spoke at a barely audible volume. "Dez, I love you. I'm sorry this is happening, and I'm sorry for how this might turn out. I'll do my best to keep this place open for you."

"Nothing can stop me, Faith. You know that. I love you, and I'll see you soon."

"Bye for now," Faith replied.

"For now," Destiny told her before hanging up.

Hays, KS

The nighttime sky glowed orange ahead, and the smell of smoke was pungent. He'd been driving for the past several hours while the others slept soundly in the back. Even Big Mac was out cold.

Connie was curled up in one of his sweatshirts in the passenger seat.

No need to wake them.

The city of Hays was on fire, there was no question of that. The flames rose a hundred feet into the air to the south of the highway. Homes and businesses along the interstate still smoldered, as if the fire had burned them earlier in the night. A fifty-foot-tall water tower was the only thing not scorched.

People stood along the left side of the highway, and he immediately recognized what they were doing, because he'd seen the Iraqis behave in a similar way when insurgents had wasted their villages.

They needed help.

I'm sorry.

The refugees hailed him like he was a giant taxi, but he dared not stop. If he did, he risked being swamped or worse by the desperate townsfolk. Once he let one person on board, hundreds of others would demand the same.

He engaged the Jake brakes to bleed off some of the dangerous speed he'd been carrying, but he still passed them at more than sixty miles an hour.

To his shock, the heat of the fire came through the glass on his left side even though the worst flames were hundreds of yards away. He couldn't imagine how the people were able to stand it.

He and his two trailing trucks stayed in the right lane, which gave them the most breathing room between the fire and them, but as he continued through the small town, people also appeared on the right side of the highway.

A crowd of hundreds had gathered right off the shoulder.

"Damn," he whispered.

A quarter of a mile later, the crowd was even thicker, as if the whole town had evacuated to the interstate. He had to slow down some more because a few children hung out close to the concrete roadway.

The CB chirped. The volume was as low as he could make it so it wouldn't wake up his family. When he answered, Monsignor was on the line.

"Buck, I'm sweeping leaves here in the back, but you should know some assholes are passing me with their lights off. Watch out."

"Roger," he replied as quietly as he could.

The fire produced enough light to see the highway without needing headlights, but he'd never turn them off while on the job. He watched his side mirror until the dark shapes came up in the lane next to him. As Monsignor warned, these jackasses had all their lights off.

"What are you guys doing?"

Six orange and white sedans rolled passed him in a tight formation, with not a single light on between them. The stenciled lettering on the sides announced they were police from Jackson, Mississippi.

They didn't slow or stop for the people of Hays, instead keeping their speed well above the legal limit of seventy-five miles per hour, almost as if they wanted to sneak by. The town was only a few miles wide, so they didn't have far to go.

When he drove out of the city limits and got away from the fire, he wasn't surprised to see the police cars turn their headlights back on. They turned on the gumball machines for good measure, then put the hammer down and raced out of view.

Why are you out here in Kansas, Mississippi?

Were the Hays police and fire department off in another state, too?

He felt bad leaving all those people, but he couldn't save a whole town on his own. There was only one thing on his mind, and it involved rescuing who he could.

He spoke softly into the CB mic. "We don't stop until Colorado."

TWENTY-ONE

Limon, CO

"Are those two still sleeping?" Connie asked Buck.

"Yep. He did good getting to me, but he spent it all."

"It's eight in the morning?"

He tapped the digital clock on his radio. "No, it's actually seven. We crossed back over into Mountain Time."

"You must go crazy crossing time zones over and over."

Buck chuckled, which was a sure sign of fatigue. He was far beyond the Federal Motor Carrier regulations for the number of consecutive hours he was allowed to drive. He had been over the limit by the time he'd made it to the truck stop in Missouri, then he'd added on another overnight shift.

It made him loopy.

"I need you to look at the atlas. Get me the shortest route to Red Mesa, Colorado."

She pulled out the book and went to the index. While she did that, she continued to chat quietly with him. "I had the worst dreams last night, and they weren't even about

Phil. I imagined I was in a gigantic fire with no hope of ever getting cool."

He thought of Hays, which was three hours behind them. Connie was supposed to be asleep, but he couldn't recall if she saw any of it.

"We all have bad dreams out here," he declared. Buck planned to prove that wrong when he finally hit the rack because he was certain he'd dream of having Garth safe with him again.

The thought of sleep made him sleepy, so he squeezed the steering wheel and really opened his eyes to let more light into his brain.

"Ah, here we go. I found it." Connie pointed to the page and traced roads with a long fingernail.

"Where do we go?"

"There's a turn-off up ahead. We go through the town of Kiowa, then we'll be at Sedalia. It takes us right to Red Mesa."

"Is it that road?"

Up ahead, an exit ramp went up to a bridge over the interstate. A lonely two-lane blacktop road went left into the grassy, rolling hills in the distance. Much like Nebraska and Wyoming, there were almost no trees from horizon to horizon.

But there were people up on the bridge.

A police car had tipped and rolled onto its roof off to the side of the exit ramp.

"Shit," he added. "The sign says this is the way to Kiowa. Are there any alternatives?"

"Not unless you want to go up into Denver, then turn south. I bet we'd hit a lot of traffic in the city."

He pulled out his lucky coin. "Here, flip this. Heads, we

get off here. Tails, we go through Denver and avoid these folks."

"Really?" she deadpanned. "You're leaving this to chance?"

"Just flip it, please."

She did as she asked, then read off the result. "Heads."

He looked at the people, the bridge, and the highway ahead. Connie glared at him sideways like he'd lost his mind.

"We exit here," he said with certainty.

He had never put too much stock in chance, so the coin was more for show. He did like it when he and the coin agreed, however.

Connie snatched up the CB mic. "I'll let those guys know where we're going."

He debated waking up Garth and Lydia but decided to let them sleep as long as possible.

Never wake a sleeping baby.

That made him laugh way more than it should.

Stay focused!

Buck studied the people as he slowed and exited onto the ramp. The police car was from somewhere in Indiana, but he went by before he could read the town name.

A young girl in a colorful summer dress ran to the side of the street, waving at him to lower his window. He had to slow anyway to make the left turn at the bridge, but he remained wary.

"Hi!" The girl waved happily like this was a charity car wash.

"Hey," he replied coolly. "We're going to Denver."

"We need a ride to Amarillo. That way." She pointed south, which wasn't the way anyone around there was going. I-70 went east and west, so she wasn't going to have much luck.

"What's in Amarillo? A boyfriend?" He hoped to keep thing civil with the girl, but some of the characters on the bridge ahead didn't look as pleasant. He wondered how she had gotten mixed up in things.

"The police dumped us on this bridge last night. Radio says we have to go to Amarillo or Cheyenne to get safe from the Godzilla monsters. We picked Amarillo because it starts with A."

His eyes nearly left their sockets, he was so surprised by her statement.

"First of all, Cheyenne is closer, so you should go there. Second, why did the police kick you out? And third, why are you going anywhere at all? Who told you there were, uh, Godzillas?"

"There was a crazy Japanese guy on the TV. He told everyone to go to Denver, but later he came on and said he discovered there were many places to get safe. Someone told us he looked scared and was constantly looking over his shoulder, like in those old monster movies, so I guess we just assumed. Anyway, Cheyenne and Amarillo were two of them he said had no monsters."

"Mon— Oh, never mind. Why did the police drop you here? Did you guys tip their car over?"

"Oh, definitely not. It was, like, there when we arrived. The police were very nice, but we wanted to get out. Denver is cold, you know? We wanted to go somewhere warm."

Buck almost ripped his face off at their stupidity, but he began to feel sorry for the girl and her friends. The twenty or thirty people on the bridge were all about her age, many dressed like they'd come from church or school. None of them had anything more substantial than a backpack, as far as he could tell.

"And all your friends got out of the police cars, too?"

"Uh huh. A nice group of state troopers picked us up on the highway and squeezed us in with other people they rescued, and then brought us out here, but we didn't want to go on. We're all from the University of Dayton, in Ohio. Go Flyers!"

A few girls on the bridge cheered with her.

These idiots are going to die out here.

"Hold on a second," he said to the girl below his window.

Buck took a moment to think, then glanced at Connie. Her face was unreadable.

"What?" he asked her.

"I can tell you have a plan. Hell, you always do, but this time I can't figure it out."

She was right, of course.

It simply took him another minute or two until he knew exactly what it was.

Limon, CO

Garth sat up in bed, aware that he wasn't moving. After being on the run for days, sitting still seemed abnormal.

"Where are we?" he asked.

The truck's cabin was empty.

"Oh."

It was daylight outside, and his head didn't feel like it was being smothered by cling wrap anymore. He figured he'd gotten a little sleep.

He slid out of bed and put on his shoes. A memory of Dad pulling them off and putting him to bed last night crept out of the darkness as if it had been stored in a deep well.

"This is what a hangover must feel like," he mumbled.

The gear from the trunk of the taxi had been piled in the rear area of the big rig's cabin. His tent, the sleeping bags, and the bottled water were all accounted for. Even his rifle and the last gun case had been shoved in there.

"Lydia!"

He shuffled to the door and flung it open.

His dad and some other people stood near the back door of the trailer. The strangers appeared to be a little older than him, many with athletic-looking backpacks, like modern-era college students. He didn't see a young woman dressed in an old-school floral dress with a bonnet, however.

Garth climbed out of the cab and was still watching the people when his foot slid on something wet and he fell to the pavement and landed awkwardly.

"Holy shit!" he blurted before he checked to see if anyone had seen his gaffe.

All clear.

The side of the truck was slathered with bug guts. Someone had cleared much of the step with a rag, but he had managed to hit enough slop to lose his footing.

It looked like someone had crunched up the insects into a mush, dumped them into an industrial mixing bucket, and then chucked the mess onto the front of his dad's truck when he was doing eighty. Some of it had splashed onto the front and sides of the trailer, although it was mostly liquid, not solids.

"Geez, Dad, where have you been driving? Hell?"

He trotted down the side of the long trailer and found Lydia. She was helping people into Buck's cargo hold. A big pile of chili cans lay next to the roadway.

"Dad, what the heck are you doing?"

Buck gave him the *big* smile, which was beyond rare. He vaguely recalled seeing such a grin when he had first learned to walk. He had gotten it when he'd shot his first rifle. Garth absolutely remembered the *big* smile when he'd brought home his first girlfriend. It was his dad's visual confirmation that he'd done something special.

"Garth!"

Buck walked over and bear-hugged him. He didn't even mind the smell of sweat and the old-man cologne his dad liked to wear. After what they'd both been through, no one smelled too good.

"I'm so glad you made it." Buck put him back down so they could talk.

"I wrecked my car," he said, disappointed.

"And you paid for it! Don't you remember? I really did it this time. I took off my belt and gave you a good whompin'!" He faked the action of side-arming a belt at him.

Garth laughed. He'd done so many things the past few days that deserved a good belting...

"No, seriously, you're here, and you're alive. I don't care if you wrecked a car doing it."

His shoulders slumped. "I'll pay to have it fixed," he told his father.

Buck guffawed. "We're way past that, son. A damaged car doesn't even register on the shit-o-meter. We're trying to stay alive here." He motioned him farther around the back of the trailer to see people climbing in.

Garth kicked one of the chili cans on the ground. "You're dropping your load?"

He and his dad snickered for a moment before Buck continued, "No, just a couple of pallets. Enough room to fit these kids. They got dumped on the side of the road and weren't going anywhere fast. They were all with the same group and there's no one else around, so I decided we could risk scooping them up. They don't know it yet, but they're going to Denver with us."

"The cops I met said they were going to Denver!"

Buck smirked. "You told me that last night."

"I did?" He wondered how much of the night would come back to him. About the only thing he remembered for certain was waking up in the front seat of the taxi and seeing Lydia smile at him. Buck might have been there, too.

"Yep. It confirmed where we had to go. I've been driving in a circle around Denver for the past two days. At first, I wanted to get away, but now it appears like it is the place to be. Something big is happening, son."

"You listened to me?"

Buck smacked him on the back of the shoulder right when a bundle of orange fur ran by.

"And you got me a dog?"

Buck gave him a thumbs-up. "We've got a lot of work to do, Garth. I'm taking these Ohio kids with us. We've got to keep moving, though, because I'm not sure how much time we have."

Garth swallowed hard. "What can I do to help?"

Buck almost let go of another *big* smile. "Your friend Lydia is assisting people into the back. I need you to make sure the front grill is clear of locust bodies. She's been running hot the past few hours, and I think it's for lack of airflow. Can you do that?"

He flashed a snappy salute. "Oorah, sir!"

Buck saluted back.

We've got this.

TWENTY-TWO

***Search for Nuclear, Astrophysical, and Krono-
metric Extremes (SNAKE). Red Mesa, Colorado***

After Faith spoke with Dez, she was interrupted by the security people. They insisted everyone prepare for the overnight hours. She was unable to make another call because the soldiers mingled in the aisles of the auditorium so small groups of people could use the restrooms.

She returned to the upstairs conference room where her managers were spending their confinement, but she arranged to have Missy summon her to the auditorium the next day.

Bob almost blew it for her. "What are you doing down there? Planning a coup?"

He'd said it loud enough for the others to hear, but no one laughed because he was still on everyone's bad side. He didn't laugh either, because his face was black and blue from the swelling in his broken nose.

"I'm taking care of my people, I'll have you know. Missy did an excellent job of keeping things going while we've been up here studying the collider issues, but now that my job is essentially over, I'd like to help where I can."

She had no intention of rolling over for Dr. Johnson and her mysterious bosses, but she wanted everyone to think that, including any asshole in the room who might decide to turn her in.

"Fine. Go." Bob seemed hurt.

On the chaperoned walk to the auditorium, she wondered if Bob was putting on an act too, or if it was all the pain from his face.

"Hello, Benny." She'd gone back to the same seat, intending to take the phone again.

"Hi, doctor. I'm not giving you the phone unless you let me report all this."

She was taken aback. "You didn't call them last night?"

He seemed sad. "No. I told you I would do this your way. I'm trying to stick to my word. But you told me you were going to make one call yesterday, and you called your sister as well. That was low, you know?"

"Don't worry. I only need to make one call right now." She was hoping to call CERN again, but she had to smooth things over with Benny first.

"My paper?"

She smiled. "Call 'em."

He dialed the number on his wife's phone while she thought over what she was going to say. She spent all night thinking about Dr. Johnson's description of SNAKE as a lifeboat. It was well-established in her mind that the time errors hadn't happened inside the sixty-two-mile circle created by the supercollider, and Mr. Shinano had broadcast that to the whole world, so why weren't people already packing in?

Why is he keeping people away from the lifeboat?

"Hello, this is Benny from Local News. Can you connect me to Mr. Hamm?" Benny leaned over and looked at his feet, the same as she'd done the previous evening. The din of numerous conversations kept the guards from hearing him talk.

Benny was silent for a time, then he chatted with someone who had to be his boss. After a minute of introductions and counter-questions, Benny handed the phone to her.

"This is Mr. Hamm. He's the editor of my department. If you have anything to share, he's your best chance."

"Thank you, Benny." He handed the live phone to her. "Hello? This is Doctor Faith Sinclair."

"Hello, Doctor. Nice to meet you. Benny has given me your background and vouched for your credentials, so I'm willing to call this conversation well-sourced. Will you be willing to talk on the record about what you are doing at the SNAKE facility?"

"Yes, but you have to broadcast this right away. People are in danger if they don't get to SNAKE as fast as possible."

"With all due respect, we already know that."

Faith was shocked. "Because of Mr. Shinano?" The Japanese businessman had talked about it on television, but she had assumed his efforts failed because there weren't crowds of people at the front door.

"Certainly. Mr. Shinano started it, and FEMA and Homeland Security have picked up the slack. Yesterday, fifty cities were added to the list of safe zones. Shinano came back on the air and confirmed that each one of them will make people immune to the unpredictable effects outside."

She still couldn't believe it. "He went back on? I'm here at SNAKE, and I haven't seen anyone except the military."

"Uh-huh," Hamm replied. "There is a giant outdoor parking and camping zone between Sedalia and the Hogback. Tens of thousands of people are there right now."

The underground collider was mostly under the foothills near Denver, but there was a portion of the loop that extended beneath the flat grasslands on the east side of the Dakota Hogback. She had always imagined that flat area as the sliver of a crescent moon because it was only a minor part of the circle under the steep hills, but if there was one place in SNAKE suitable for parking cars and rescuing a crowd of humanity, it was there.

"Well, I wanted to tell people we have three hundred square miles of land inside the safe zone of the loop. The entire population of America could fit here if we had the time."

Feeding them and sheltering them would be next to impossible, but she was confident everyone could ride out the storm for a short time.

"Very interesting, Doctor. I'll pass that along. What else can you tell us? Communications have been wrecked across America, so getting the message to the people has been left to the biggest stations still broadcasting with government approval. It might be tough for us to provide counter-programming."

"You have to try," she said as loud as she dared. "SNAKE is safe. I'm not sure about the other locations you mentioned, but Shinano was right about this one. We are safe, and there is plenty of room for more, okay?"

"We'll pass it along," Hamm said in a tired voice.

She remembered who had made the call possible. "I also want it on record Benny was here during most of this incident. He can give you a full account of what's been going on with the SNAKE supercollider, and the concurrent experiment running between our facility and the one in Switzerland."

That gave her an idea.

"I have a phone number I want to give you. This is the direct link to CERN. You should be able to talk to a Dr. Kyle Johnson about the rips in time created by an illicit project called Four Arrows."

A light came on in her brain, and she suddenly saw how she could fight back.

"And let me give you another phone number. It will all make sense when you talk to both of these people."

Red Mesa, CO

"Sir, this isn't right. Those cars are being corralled to the wrong location. I'm sure of it." Phil and Ethan stood in dense cover near the top of a hill overlooking the Hogback and the plains beyond. To the left, metropolitan Denver appeared to be painted onto the flat plains from the hump of the Hogback all the way to the horizon. A small town was straight out, and a huge parking lot had sprung up beyond it.

"What do you want us to do about it?" Ethan asked.

"Sir, we give Private Sanchez and the other two airmen pistols to cover the prisoners, liberate some transport, and we go down there and un-fuck this horseshit. I don't know if they're telling the truth about being with the 130th Division or if we're living in some sort of screwed up parallel reality, but the fact is that these assholes know they are safe on top of the disc created by the supercollider ring. However, based on what Murphy drew as a boundary to keep himself safe, it's clear the curve doesn't go beyond that little town." He pointed to the twinkling of glass and chrome far out on the grassy plains.

"It's still not our lane."

"Ethan, our mission was to shut down a facility on the other side of the world. We're never getting back there. All of America's troops are coming home, and they said it was to protect our country from this time-travel insanity. Well, we're here. We can protect those people—our people—right now."

The Lieutenant Colonel shook his head as he looked down. "I haven't been able to raise anyone on the outside to confirm our success, but we performed the mission to the best of our ability. The power was off before we left Switzerland. You saw it."

"I concur."

"And you and I also agree that something is fishy about this unit. I don't feel compelled to jump into the chain of command of an Army division that should not exist."

"One hundred percent agree."

Ethan shrugged. "Well, as long as we are already here, this seems like as worthy a cause as any. Get the men together."

"We're going?" he pressed.

"Task Force Blue 7 rides again."

Coral Sea, Pacific Ocean

"Zandre, before we go in, I have to say I don't think this is going to end well." She had shared the basics of her phone call with Faith. She knew her sister well enough to know they didn't have three weeks to cross the ocean. Her last play was to ask the captain if he could go any faster.

"We can only do what we can do, mate. If the captain tells us it's over, then at least we tried."

She passed through the door to the bridge. Many of her colleagues from the Sydney Harbor Foundation were already inside, as if they wanted to share in the duties of leadership. It was a sentiment she understood since the administration staff spent most of their time ordering peons like her to various animal hotspots rather than doing it themselves.

"Welcome! I'm Captain Keith Barlow."

The captain reminded her of the actor who played the captain in that movie about the *Titanic*. He had the same white hair and long beard, although he was larger and rounder than the character in the movie.

"Thanks for letting me come in."

"Of course. We're all lucky the SHF team managed to get us out of Sydney before things got worse."

They even took credit for my warning.

Before hearing any other bad news, she blurted, "We have to go faster."

Laughter tittered around the room.

She went on, "I talked to my sister in Colorado. She's the one who warned me the world was ending. When I told her it would take us weeks to cross the ocean, she had a fit. Captain, uh, sir, we have to go faster."

He put his hands on a piece of equipment that looked like a handle sticking out of a box. "We are already traveling at the maximum safe cruising speed. They told me this was an emergency, and I've treated it as such."

"Can't you squeeze more out of the engines? They do it all the time in the movies." There were no icebergs in the South Pacific, although she briefly thought of the creature they'd struck on the way out of Sydney. It had seemed as big as one.

"Miss, we have enough fuel for thirty-four days at almost maximum speed. It should only take us about twenty to reach Los Angeles. From there, the SHF people have assured me passage to Colorado. I'm not going to do anything to risk that, okay?"

Her soul flooded with disappointment. "Yeah, mate, I hear you."

I'm sorry, sis. I'm pretty sure I'm not going to make it.

Kiowa, CO

Buck used the Jakes to reduce speed through the town of Kiowa. It was a typical one-stoplight town, but without the stoplight. The two-lane main street was about a mile long, with lots of trees and a few Victorian homes along the sides.

Horses were tied up in front of a place resembling a saloon.

"I think we've found my home," Connie said with excitement.

"You'd live in a place like this?" Buck lived on Staten Island, which was more or less a crowded, never-ending subdivision. Kiowa had as many people as one city block back home. "There isn't much to do but watch the traffic go by."

"After this journey, that's exactly what I want to do—find a home where the most important decision I have to make is where on the wraparound porch I'm going to sit and relax."

"These look like houses from my time," Lydia said from the rear of the cabin.

"Would you live in one?" Garth asked her.

"Oh, certainly. These people are obviously rich, to live in such luxury."

Buck only saw them as drains on his underfunded pocketbook. There were so many windows on the fancy homes, he figured they'd need an air conditioner unit for each one. After spending time touring the Middle East, cool air was one luxury he didn't know if he could live without. That was why he kept his cabin so cold.

"If you fine people could live in a drafty old house like these, I'm in."

Connie laughed. "Are you saying you'd be willing to settle down? You'd put the truck in Park permanently?"

He was certain she was joking about it, but he'd been thinking that very thing almost since the first blast of blue energy went overhead. He'd desperately wanted to get back to Garth and have things return to normal, but his son was with him now, and opportunity beckoned him to do more than return to how things were. He wanted to spend real time with him. It was easy to see Garth and Big Mac running around in the grassy green yards of the big houses they were passing.

And if Connie was there, so much the better.

Lydia can live next door.

Buck's Peterbilt rolled through the town in about two minutes. His fantasy ended when six motorcycles roared passed and got in front of him.

Connie tensed.

"Be ready," he said, worried.

TWENTY-THREE

Kiowa, CO

"You know those guys?" Garth asked from the back.

Connie seemed so surprised to see the bikers, he almost believed they were the same ones they'd tangled with in California. However, they were dressed in black leather and jeans without any of the gang patches worn by the Trash Pandas.

"No," Buck said with relief. "They're normal bikers."

"Thank God." Connie looked back at Garth. "Your father and I met when he rescued me from some motorcycle badasses like them."

"Nah, they weren't badasses. They were just asses. They wouldn't let me back up my truck ten feet. Can you believe that? If they'd given me ten feet, they'd still be alive."

"You killed them?" Garth seemed impressed.

"Forget about it," he groused. A second later, he realized he'd been abrupt. "Sorry. I'm about tapped out."

"Believe me, I understand." Garth reached into the supplies piled at his feet. "Here, drink this."

"Mountain Dew?"

"Tons of caffeine. It helped get me most of the way across Missouri."

"I love that drink!" Lydia stated in a bubbly voice.

"Yeah, but you have to pace yourself. I gave her some, and she almost bounced out the car window, she was so hopped up on caffeine."

"Thanks, son. I'll try not to bounce." Connie opened it for him so he could keep his hands on the wheel.

"It's the least I can do," Garth added.

He and Connie watched the bikers drive off into the distance while Garth and Lydia talked quietly in the sleeper. Big Mac seemed to enjoy lying between the two kids, and he wasn't about to suggest the dog move.

A few minutes later, a huge military transport flew low and slow over Buck's left shoulder. It was on the same path as them.

"Gee, I wonder where they're going?" he asked sarcastically.

"Seems like the whole world is heading to SNAKE," Connie answered.

"I thought the planes were grounded?" Garth put forth from the back.

"Nobody tells the military what to do," Buck replied.

They watched the four-propeller giant until the warped landscape blocked it from their view, much like the bikers.

They made good time as they headed west. The terrain was relatively flat, with some hills and creek beds, so it was easy driving. However, when they started to see the foothills ahead, traffic started to stack up, and their pace dropped to match.

Eve's voice came from the CB. "Hey, Buck. Sparky says to turn on the radio. Big news."

Connie did the honors.

A woman was already talking. "...and that is only the first step. You must stay inside the circle of the SNAKE supercollider when the power is cut. If you remain outside the circle, you risk being swept up by the overflow of dark energy from the severed link."

The voice paused.

"Is she done?" Connie asked as the woman came back.

"I don't know if the government is able to assure your safety in the cities they say are safe. I hope they are telling the truth. However, you should know an Army unit came to Red Mesa, Colorado last night and took over. Their reason for coming here wasn't to keep us safe or fix the collider. Instead, they came here because they believed this is the only place they can be safe from the impending disaster."

"I knew it!" Buck blurted out. "That military convoy was going to the supercollider. It wasn't to take it over, though. It was to survive."

"Shh," Connie replied.

The radio voice carried on. "I'm sorry for the delay in doing this, but my technical capabilities are very limited while I'm trapped by the Army in here. However, the studio says they are calling two people who can verify everything I'm telling you."

A string of clicks and chimes rang out from the radio.

"Hello?" a man asked as if he was part of a radio call-in show.

A second man with a similar voice said, "Who is this?"

"Hello, gentlemen. You both know me. I'm Doctor Faith Sinclair, head of Search for Nuclear, Astrophysical, and Kronometric Extremes in Red Mesa, CO."

"How do you have a phone?" one of the men

complained with anger and surprise. "And who else is on the line? This is a security breach of the highest order."

The woman didn't skip a beat. "I've linked you two together because it is important you both know what the other is doing. Doctor Kyle Johnson is on the line in Geneva, Switzerland. Say hello, please."

One of the men did so.

"And also on the line, I have the current leader of the SNAKE supercollider. You took over the entire campus as a way to save us, didn't you, Doctor Kyle Johnson? Why don't you say hello too?"

"What the hell is this?" angry Kyle responded.

"This isn't possible," nice Kyle added, "but it does sound like me."

The woman spoke fast. "There are two Dr. Johnsons on the line, but they aren't twins or brothers or even related. They are the same person. A failed experiment at CERN in Switzerland sent a carbon copy of the man over here to America."

Buck and Connie looked at each other as if they were listening to a science fiction program. It wasn't possible to be two places at once.

"This is crazy," Buck said reverently.

"I know," she mouthed.

"Ladies and gentlemen of America, please be aware Dr. Johnson could have gone anywhere in the world after he traveled the quantum bridge between Switzerland and Colorado. Anywhere. And yet he chose to come here. That's because—"

"Wait! Stop! Is this being broadcast?" Angry Kyle grew even more distraught. "How are you doing this, Faith? Someone, stop her!"

The determined woman did not stop. "He's mad

because he knows SNAKE is the only place on this side of the world he can be safe when his people drop a nuclear bomb on Geneva, Switzerland. That's how he plans to fix the world."

"No!"

The woman chuckled. "Please, everyone listening to this. Get to Red Mesa, Colorado. I don't know if it is going to be permanently safe or if the security will be temporary, but I swear to you on this radio program that you and your family will have a better chance than if—"

Screams bleated from the radio, and the woman stopped talking. After more shouting, snaps of sound cracked out of the speakers.

"Gunshots," Buck deadpanned.

"Holy shit," Garth exclaimed. "This is intense."

A new voice came on the frequency. "We will try to rejoin Dr. Sinclair as soon as possible. In the meantime, we have an updated list of safe cities."

The radio broadcast was over.

More traffic stacked up in front of them.

"Welcome to Sedalia," Connie relayed as they passed the sign.

Red Mesa, CO

Once Phil had Ethan's support, he sprang to action with a plan. As he suggested, the three NORAD airmen were assigned to watch over the two captured guards, while the six enlisted and two officers from Task Force Blue 7 made their way out of the hills and down to the Hogback.

They kept out of the way of the soldiers and wandered into an upscale subdivision with plenty of available vehicles to requisition. They decided to take four cars, two men per vehicle, leaving him with Corporal Grafton again. On a whim, he cut an American flag off a subdivision flag pole before they got on the road.

"Where are we going?" Grafton asked as Phil drove the borrowed pickup truck down the narrow two-lane road. Based on his reconnaissance, the road would take them between two of the steep sections of Hogback and onto the flat plains.

"I saw a town at the edge of the ring." He wished he had his full battalion with him again. He hadn't seen them since his injury and evac out of Afghanistan. There were so many people in danger that he needed more than one man to help him. "We'll get all those people to come up this road. Damn, sure would have been nice to have your radio for this."

"Truth. The 130ᵗʰ guys could have brought people up here at any time, though. Why didn't they?"

He didn't want to guess, but he couldn't stop himself. It could have been intentional, or it could have been an oversight. Just as likely, it was some incompetent officer who had handed out the wrong marching orders. Phil could easily fix the error by going down there and making people go where he wanted.

It took five minutes to get to the designated area of operations. As he thought, the tiny town of Sedalia was the boundary between the outline of the supercollider and the rest of the Colorado high plains. The canyon road went into town from the west, an intersecting two-lane highway that ran roughly north-south, forming a crude T-shape.

"They are putting people outside the collider." On the far side of the main highway, above the T, cars were being directed into a huge field by soldiers almost certainly from the 130ᵗʰ.

There was nothing but empty fields on the near side of

the highway, below the top of the T. To his left, several guards stood by a small concrete blockhouse, which was the familiar emergency exit portal he recognized from the woods. Another bunker was barely visible about two miles down the highway. The second one was also on the near side of the road, giving him visual confirmation of what he already suspected.

"You see this T-shape? Everything in town and on this side of the highway is safe. Everything on the far side of the highway is in danger." Phil pulled the pickup to the side of the road.

A ten-foot-tall deer fence ran for miles along the highway. The only break in it was the few blocks of the rustic village. Many soldiers crowded the roads in the town, and they had dozens of Humvees clogging the streets and acting as roadblocks.

No one was allowed through the town. Instead, they were directed to the growing parking area beyond the highway. It was still unclear how the order had gotten messed up, but he had a better sense of how to fix it now.

"What do we do?"

"Grafton, this might get you into major trouble. Possibly shot. I don't know what those boys over there are going to do once we kick this off, so you don't have to come with me if you don't want."

Grafton motioned to the crowds. "My wife might be out there. She lives in Pueblo. If there's any chance she is, I want to get her to safety. If not, and she's waiting in some other line, I'd hope there would be someone willing to do the right thing. I'm down for whatever."

He put the truck into gear and turned right into the scrub-grass field next to the canyon road. The plan was to avoid the town of Sedalia in the middle of the action and go to the southern flank of the crowd. It would keep him as far from the soldiers as possible. Grafton held onto their rifles, but there was almost no point in having them since there were dozens of soldiers in the town and only two of them.

The rest of Task Force Blue 7 was supposed to go to other parts of the collider ring, but after seeing the situation up close, Phil realized that all three groups should have converged on the town. That was where all the action was.

When he was a mile from Sedalia, he turned and aimed the truck toward the fence.

The hot, dusty two-lane roadway evoked memories of his mother for some reason. She had disappeared on a dusty Nevada highway, so it wasn't unusual to think of her when the conditions were similar.

Stay in the present, Phil.

Almost no one on the packed highway seemed to notice him.

He had an idea for how to change that.

Sedalia, CO

Garth leaned against Buck's seat so he could see all the action outside. Cars and trucks scooted into the fields to the right, parking where they could.

"This is it?" he asked.

"I don't know," Buck replied. "Connie? Are we there already?"

His dad's friend flipped through the road atlas until she found the Colorado map. "No, definitely not. This is Sedalia, which is pretty far from Red Mesa. I don't think we should stop here."

"The radio said we have to get into the area protected

209

by the SNAKE collider. I don't see anything that looks remotely scientific out here."

Aside from a random concrete shack behind a deer fence, he hadn't seen any trace of civilization along the remote highway. There was a small town up ahead and the cars in the field, but not much else.

The radio broadcaster stopped reading the names of cities and spoke directly to the audience. "Ladies and gentlemen, we regret we couldn't continue with Dr. Sinclair's live broadcast from inside the SNAKE facility, but we can confirm the part of what she said was true. Shortwave radio tells of a nuclear strike in the mountains of Switzerland. We have no other details at this time, but we believe it corroborates her story."

Buck exhaled loudly.

Garth shared his anxiety. "Are we safe here?"

They were stuck in a huge traffic jam, but lots of cars were turned into the grass on the right side of the road, getting into any open space they could, and following what everyone else was doing.

"This isn't Red Mesa, Buck," Connie drawled.

He mumbled the F-word under his breath. "There is something wrong here, but I can't figure it out."

Connie pointed to the west. "We want to be in those hills."

"Then let's go," Garth encouraged everyone. "We don't have to do what everyone else is doing."

Buck looked all around, then raised the CB microphone. "This is Buck. We're figuring out where to go next—"

Lydia pointed across his face, out Buck's window. "What's that man doing?"

A soldier had crashed his sand-colored truck through the long, wire fence. While they watched, he jumped out of his rig, grabbed an American flag, and started waving it like one of those guys who swing around big plastic arrows to announce new stores at the mall.

"Dad, look at him!" He tapped the side window so his dad knew where to look.

He stopped talking on the CB and briefly looked at Connie. Her taut smile made up his mind.

"Hold on, guys," he said to his cab mates. "I don't know what this is about, but I'd rather take my chances on the side of the highway closest to the mountains than follow all these people to the wrong parking lot."

Traffic had been stopped for a while and Buck didn't have much room in front of him, but he turned anyway.

"Right on, Dad," Garth encouraged him.

Garth smiled at Lydia, then grabbed her hand. "I told you my dad knows what he's doing. He won't let us down."

Buck gave it a little gas and turned left, causing the Peterbilt's front bumper to tap the car in front of them. A few seconds later, he was free of the line of cars, and he drove off the far shoulder and into the weedy field in front of the fence.

"I trust you and your nice father." Lydia smiled.

To his surprise, she grabbed Big Mac's collar and pulled the Golden close as if to protect him.

Please don't disappear.

TWENTY-FOUR

Search for Nuclear, Astrophysical, and Krono-metric Extremes (SNAKE). Red Mesa, Colorado

After the guards had unloaded warning shots, she'd had to throw the phone on the ground to smash it. She didn't want to implicate Benny, even though his newspaper was clearly involved. Minutes later, she was dragged into the main control room of the collider, where Dr. Johnson was waiting for her.

"Faith, I'm very disappointed in you. How could you not know I would figure out where you were? You weren't even hiding. From what I gather, you've done a good job of keeping this operation running during our overtime scenario, but this trashes all of it."

She laughed in Dr. Johnson's face. "Is that what you call this? Your experiment won't stop running on my collider, and you think this is overtime?"

"*Your* collider? You obviously don't know who pays the bills."

The government had had a hand in the preliminary financing and construction, but she believed private money, like Azurasia Heavy Industries, had powered most of the science once the facility was running. However, she couldn't deny that many things had been hidden from her.

"You've just destroyed a billion-dollar facility and the people who ran it. How can you stand there and lecture me about anything?" She tried to spit in his face, but it wasn't in her skill set and her spittle missed by a mile.

The pudgy man used both hands to wipe his whole face as if she had landed a direct hit. "You have no idea what's going on out there, but know this. Your little stunt of having me talk to myself did nothing but speed up this process."

"It wasn't a stunt," she broke in. "The other man was you. I talked to him twice. He's you in a timeline where you aren't a prick who runs projects your peers don't know about. If you'd listened to him, he could have helped you solve the problem you created here."

"Stop!" Dr. Johnson barked. "He was *not* me. And even if he was, he's gone. I was told just now that five nuclear-tipped Cruise missiles crossed the Alps from one of our ships in Italy. They wiped Geneva and everything under it right off the map."

She fell hard into one of the plastic chairs in the control room where she'd been brought.

"I failed?"

"Totally," the man replied. "CERN is gone. I don't know how you could possibly argue with me, but we are now safe."

She looked up with concern, her analytical mind refusing to ignore the details. "Are the beams off? Are we unlinked? How long ago was the attack?"

"A couple of minutes. The press picked it up on short-wave and blabbed it on the radio almost in real time, the bastards. They can't keep anything quiet. That was why we forced Shinano to recant and lead people astray."

She didn't know who he meant, but she watched as he turned on a video screen.

"Now," he went on, "we get to see if the cost was worth it."

The monitor had four feeds on it, like a split screen with four shows running at the same time. The top left was a view of the Four Arrows box. The blue light linking it to CERN was still lit, suggesting the link was still there.

The top right box showed a black screen.

Dr. Johnson pointed to the blackness. "That's CERN."

The bottom right was a blue reservoir surrounded by green trees. She recognized it as one of the foothill lakes on top of SNAKE. There was nothing out of the ordinary on the image.

The bottom left screen was also easy to identify as the town of Sedalia. One highway ran through town on the east side, and a few blocks of houses were to the west. It was even smaller than when they went through Kiowa. However, it looked like Woodstock had come for a visit, because a huge number of cars were parked in the fields to the east of the village.

That caught her immediate attention. "They are parking outside the collider ring. Why are they outside?"

He didn't turn to look at where she pointed.

"We control everything, Faith. This facility only has limited supplies, plus what we brought for ourselves. I'd love to save all those people, but they're only going to be a drag on us if we let every single one of them inside. It's more humane to cut the cord now, at the beginning."

"I have to warn them," she implored. "Get them to safety, like you said."

She'd spent all her time cooped up inside the science lab while everyone else suffered on the outside. It seemed like a cruel twist of the knife that she was destined to survive solely because of dumb luck, while those outside were slated to die because of the vile act of an uncaring scientist.

Faith casually turned toward the door, wondering if she could make a run for it, but was stunned to see six or seven soldiers watching her from beyond the threshold.

General Smith would say go for it.

"You are out of the game, Doctor," he said with mock sadness, perhaps sensing her internal dilemma. "I brought you up here to show you I was right."

"We could have easily saved all those people until the time anomaly cleared up."

He furrowed his eyebrows. "I hope you understand that I'm trying to save the best and the brightest for what comes next. This isn't just the end of the experiment, it's the beginning of a new world."

"That sounds like the ravings of a lunatic."

"I didn't show you everything in the film with the laser beam and the lead plate. I cut it off before the final frames because I didn't think your peers were ready for it. I don't have a projector on my person, but would you like me to give you the punchline?"

She watched the video feed of Sedalia. The image began to dance and jitter as if an electrical charge was interfering with the screen.

"Sure. Why not."

"About fifty yards behind the man standing at the lead plate, there is an arboretum on the property of Malmstrom Air Base. Several of the plants and trees within the direct path of that laser experiment exploded with growth. Some punched through the clear roof in a matter of minutes."

She was awestruck at another potential benefit for mankind. Instant growth of food-bearing plants and trees could save billions of lives from starvation.

"Do you know what that means?"

She rolled her eyes. "I'm sure you're going to tell me."

"I am," he said in a businesslike manner. "It means that the change state of the outer edge of the energy pulse does not reverse itself when the main source is discontinued."

Faith understood his tech talk.

"Oi. You've got to be kidding me."

"I'm not."

He wasn't lying. It really *was* a punchline. "Nothing is ever going back to the way it was," she suggested.

"I told you, this place is a lifeboat. Everything outside the ring of your collider will cease to exist in about—" He looked at his watch. "Now."

She turned back to the video feed.

Something was happening outside.

Sedalia, CO

Phil felt like he was starring in a movie about the Civil War. He waved the American flag for all he was worth, and somewhere nearby there were enemy soldiers who wouldn't take kindly to his brash action. It would be worth it, though, if he could save some lives.

"Come on!" he yelled to the civilians. "This way!"

The highway was filled with idling vehicles waiting to turn right into the fields of parked cars. He only needed a few of the mobile ones to come his way and start a new line to the left so those still on the road would follow.

The first vehicle out of the line was a large black tractor-trailer that looked like it been splashed with tar while doing a hundred miles an hour. The driver angled the big rig out of line and drove deliberately toward the fence.

Too late, he realized the hole he'd made with the pickup wasn't going to be wide enough for the giant truck.

He waved his arms faster, hoping the driver knew what he meant.

"Just go through!" he screamed.

Like any good ol' boy, the guy laid on his horn as he gunned the motor. He made no effort to slow but went directly through the fence, knocking down one of the wooden posts holding up the ten-foot-tall wire mesh.

"Shit, yeah!" he screamed.

Phil stepped back to give the trucker plenty of room to plow on through, and he thought he saw the face of a familiar-looking woman riding shotgun. She wore a toothy white smile, as if she were enjoying a thrilling roller coaster ride.

"Welcome to salvation, lady!"

He turned to Grafton, who had scooted into the driver's seat of the pickup truck.

"Open up more sections, okay? I'm going to wave people in." Phil pointed toward town, which was where he wanted to break down the fence.

A few seconds after the black truck went through, a little blue spark shot out of the broken fence and arced over to the top of the borrowed pickup truck. The "zzt" sound of electricity made him hop back.

At first, he thought maybe the fence was electrified, but the tendrils of blue began to appear on and between vehicles parked on the highway.

"Holy hell, it's happening now!"

Murphy's words came haunting back into his mind. "I don't want to disappear."

How much time do I have?

He'd trained all his life to protect the people of the United States. Sitting in guard towers in remote locations in Afghanistan sometimes made him question his usefulness to individual citizens, but this was the exact opposite. Thousands of his countrymen now depended on him to step into the breach.

Phil imagined that was literal. He stood near the gap he'd created by running down the first bit of fence. There was a larger hole where the semi had punched through.

Now he had to get people to follow.

"Fucking Rangers lead the way!"

He ran for the highway.

Sedalia, CO

Buck drove the truck about a hundred yards into the scrubby field.

"This should be far enough." He put on the brakes and stopped.

"Why here?" Garth asked.

"I wanted to give the other cars enough room to follow us through."

It didn't appear as if many drivers had followed them. Cars were coming through, but they stayed closer to the fence line. He also noticed something else.

"Shit, there's blue fire back there. That's the energy I saw in the sky when all this started." The outline of the sparks ran along the fence line next to the road and curved away from the parked cars on the other side. It appeared as if the soldier with the pickup truck knew the rescue effort was FUBAR and wanted to make things right.

"What does it mean, darlin'?" Connie drawled.

Buck hesitated when he looked at his girlfriend. He wondered if his son was thinking the same thing as him.

Is this the end of Connie and Lydia?

"Stay here," Buck yelled. He opened his door and flew out.

About two seconds later, someone slammed the passenger door.

You crazy woman.

Connie ran to the gap between the tractor and trailer, hopped onto the fifth-wheel frame, then ran across it to be with him. He met her when she sat on the edge.

"Buck, I don't know what's going on, but I think this is the big one. The woman on the radio said we're safe, but I don't know if that includes me. I just wanted to say..."

"This isn't that!" he protested.

She shushed him. "Just kiss me, you goofy Marine."

He intended to, even leaned in for it, but he briefly glanced at the frothing blue light again. Before she opened her eyes, he gave her a quick peck on the lips. When that was all, she grabbed his Hawaiian shirt, intent on more.

He pulled back. "Connie, this isn't the end, I promise you. I think we were shown the way by that Army dude because we're supposed to do more than sit here and celebrate."

Her eyes broadcast a brief look of confusion until she got on the same wavelength. "You want to help those people?"

A few cars and pedestrians were running through the two holes in the fence, but a city's worth of vehicles was still parked beyond the roadway. The Army guy was still there waving his flag, but someone drove his truck down the fence and created a third hole. He looked like a mouse taking bites out of a sequoia, there was so much fence left.

"I know how we can do it. I'm going to unhook the trailer. You open the back and get those college kids out. Tell them the price of freedom is bringing more people to this side of the road. I'm going to do my part with the Peterbilt." He let her go and popped off the pigtail connections between the tractor and box trailer, then scooted underneath the trailer to unhitch the kingpin.

"Buck, don't be the hero, you hear me?" She spoke in a stern voice he couldn't recall her using before.

"Connie, I can't let that Army asshole save all those people by himself. I'll get beat up at the VFW hall if this is how my story gets told."

He spoke in an old-man voice. "Your Granpap was a Marine, by Jove, but he preferred to sit on his ass and let some weak-ass ditch-digger get all the glory while he polished his—"

"Okay, I get it." She laughed.

"I'm not wearing a uniform, but I've got to show him up." He laughed to hide his feelings about the danger level of what he had in mind.

"Charlie Mike," she said with a mix of disappointment and pride.

"I won't do anything stupid," he assured her, not knowing if he could possibly live up to that promise.

Probably not.

"Oh, and if the college kids ask, tell them this is Amarillo!"

He snickered at the look of horror on her face.

TWENTY-FIVE

Sedalia, CO

Buck unhooked the kingpin and detached the trailer in record time. Without a trailer, his semi-truck was free to go bobtail-style, which made him more maneuverable.

Don't do anything stupid, he reminded himself.

"Garth? Where are you?"

He and Lydia came around the front bumper holding hands. The furtive look he flashed at the pioneer girl next to him was precisely how he felt about Connie when she took off for the rear of the trailer.

He thinks she's going away, too.

Buck pointed away from his rig. "Guys, go stand over there. I'm going back to the fence to help the rest of those people."

"But Dad, it's already started!"

His heart skipped a beat, knowing he was putting himself in danger, but as long as Garth was safe behind the finish line, he had to live up to his own code of honor. He'd never forgive himself if he sat idle while people suffered a hundred yards away.

"Trust me, this has to happen!"

He hopped up and reached for his door handle, but Garth came over and held him back. At first, he thought it was because he wanted to stop him, but he realized it wasn't that at all.

Garth gave him an awkward hug. "Thanks for saving us, Dad. Go get 'em, but be sure to bring yourself back."

Buck hugged him for a second, then gently pushed him away. Lydia was close by, smiling, so he spoke to her as he climbed into the cab. "Take care of him, okay? Don't let him out of your sight!"

"I will!" she said as if she'd been given a task she very much wanted.

He got the Peterbilt started, amazed by how messy she had become over the past several days. The outside was a disaster, with the blanket of locusts only being the last in a long line of things splashed and wiped on the paint. However, the inside was a wreck now too. They'd tracked in dirt, rocks, and bug slop over the last thousand miles. Garth's things were piled in the back, with all the organization of the front lawn of a rural mobile home.

"I need a name for you," he said to the cabin as he turned the truck around. "I'm not going to call you Locust, because that's not pretty. How about Lorraine? It's an L-name and sounds fancy." Buck's policy was never to name his vehicles because he didn't like saying goodbye to inanimate objects after he'd been with them for a long time, but he would make this exception because the Peterbilt had treated him so well. She deserved special recognition.

"All right, Lorraine, we're rolling hot."

Buck passed Eve and Monsignor as he headed back to the fence line. Neither had unhitched their trailers, so he didn't expect any help from them. It wasn't a knock, he reasoned, because he hadn't known what he was going to do until the last second, either.

Far to the left, Humvees flew out of the town of Sedalia like angry hornets coming to defend the hive. Some came along the line of fencing, while others went toward his trailer.

"You're too late," he said, hoping he was right.

The blue sparks had grown in the short time since they began. The deer fence was crackling with lots of energy, but so were some of the cars on the roadway beyond it.

"Don't pass out, Buck." The energy wave reminded him of what had happened back in Wyoming when everyone around him fainted. Now he was heading into an electrical storm.

He blared his horn as he bounced over the field.

The soldier with the flag waved people through the hole he'd created, and some cars came through the gap Buck had opened, but it wasn't enough. Traffic was piled up as far as he could see on the highway, and most of them likely had no idea what was taking place at that one section of fence.

Riding the horn the whole way, he turned into the barrier and knocked over the closest wooden fence post. Without his heavy payload, the impact with the four-inch piece of wood slowed him down a bit. However, he dumped Lorraine into a lower gear and headed directly for the next one.

Blue ripples of electricity came out of his dashboard, and he held his breath like its presence was going to knock him out, but he remained conscious as he drove Lorraine into another tall post. It cracked and fell over like he'd tackled it on the football field.

Before he hit the next one, he rolled down his window and waved at the people on the road.

"Come this way!" he shouted.

Lorraine bashed the next post with a loud thwack, but something slammed into his undercarriage as he rolled over it.

"Fuck!"

For a few seconds, he thought something was damaged and he almost stalled out, but he figured it was all or nothing, so he gave it more power.

"This way!" Buck waved like a maniac.

He peered into the side mirror, happy to see that some cars were turning as he instructed.

A familiar figure caught his eye, however. Garth had hopped across the downed fence and now ran across the highway. Blue sparks chased him the whole way.

"What are you doing, son?"

Sedalia, CO

Garth watched Buck drive away in the bobtail semi-truck, but he wasn't content to sit and watch. Though it might have been comforting to let his dad take over all responsibilities and go back to being the dutiful child, he didn't feel that way anymore. He and Lydia had worked as a team the past few days, and he didn't want to give it all up.

"I've got to help those people," he suggested.

Lydia stood next to him, watching the traffic.

The other two trucks in the convoy had pulled close to their trailer, and Connie and her Golden Retriever were helping those kids come down from the back, which left the two of them more or less alone in the wild grass.

"We can run over there," she offered, "but how do we get them to come here?"

He didn't know, but it was as good a plan as any.

"Run with me, okay?"

She tightened her bonnet like a race was about to begin, and they took off together.

They crossed the field in a couple of minutes, and they had the perfect perspective to watch Buck use his truck to plow over the posts and rip the deer fence to shreds as he widened the entrance to the field.

"That's perfect!" he shouted. "We only have to show people the way, and they'll drive or walk through."

"I hope you're right." With less confidence, she added, "That blue light scares me."

"Don't worry about it. Those people are already in it. Dad is in it. I don't think it can hurt you."

In the back recesses of his mind, he worried she might get swept away inside the blue energy, the same way she'd been delivered to him. However, he did his best to ignore that so he could do what he planned.

"Come on!"

Garth ran and jumped over a twisted piece of the wire fence. A spark of blue electricity nipped at his leg, giving him a tingly feeling.

Oh, shit!

It was too late to change his plans. He ran through the fence and continued onto the roadway. As soon as he was near the parked cars, he started to yell. "Go over there! You are on the wrong side!"

Lydia followed him a second or two later, but they shared a look of concern. "I'm going over there." Lydia pointed to cars closer to the town. He knew they'd save more people by splitting up, but it started to make him worry.

More electricity bubbled out of the ground by the fence.

"Okay, but don't take long!" He flashed her a brave

smile, wondering if he was doing the right thing. Was he being the hero or putting his friend in mortal danger?

"I won't!" she said as she ran off.

As she did, several of the students from his dad's trailer came across the road.

"That cowgirl woman sent us after you," one of the young women cried. "How can we help?"

"Just tell people to run across this road. Everyone we can get on this side—" Garth pointed to the side with the fence, "will be safe."

It was impossible to know what was coming, but the blue sparks were a lot like those he'd seen on the first day. If things were going back to normal on the far side of the fence, that was where he had to be.

The students all spread out into the mass of parked cars, and panicky throngs immediately began running out of the lot. More and more people trotted across the road, giving him confirmation that they were making a difference.

Two policewomen ran up to him, each holding a baby. "They told us to come to SNAKE, and we thought this was it. We're asking for our unit. Will we be safe over there? Why is everyone on this side?"

Garth waved them on. "Don't take any chances! SNAKE runs under those hills, so how could it be on this side of the road but not the other?" He'd been listening to the radio, and his dad and Connie had talked about the giant ring under the earth. All they knew for sure was Red Mesa was west of Sedalia, so they based everything on geography.

He briefly recalled Officer Jones, back in Columbia, telling him he needed to work on his geography. In ten million years, he never would have thought that knowledge would save his life.

"Trust me!" he shouted over the traffic noise. The truck's horn was going off every few seconds, although he was far down the road now.

"That adds up," the officer replied. After talking on a hand-held radio, both women ran for the fence.

Garth took off into the endless parking lot of cars, trying to find people who hadn't been swayed by the college kids ahead of him. A troubling number of gawkers stood around watching. Many were curious to see the idiot in the semi knocking over the fence like it was a video game.

"Tell everyone!" he shouted to the closest people. "Get to the other side of the fence! You are on the wrong side!"

For a moment, they stood there like deer frozen in headlights, but the college students were shouting the same thing. They'd run up other aisles of cars, and the yelling came from multiple directions.

We're all in, right or wrong.

He trusted that his dad knew what he was doing. He wouldn't risk his life or his precious truck if he didn't believe this was the right course of action.

Garth ran deeper into the field of cars until something caught him by the leg.

"What the hell?"

He looked down to find Big Mac nipping at his jeans as if desperate to get him to stop running.

There was at least a mile of parked cars ahead of him, and lots of people had already set up blankets and pillows on top of their vehicles to wait it out. However, word of mouth caught many of the bystanders like a virus spreading across the field, so lots of runners came back down the long aisles. That was great, but there were so many people left to save...

Mac came around to his front and gave him an urgent nudge.

"I don't believe it," Garth exhaled. "Did my dad send you?"

Impossible. Buck was still honking and demolishing fence.

"It's time to go back, isn't it, Big Mac?"

The Golden barked, then trotted toward the fence. He paused a few yards away as if making sure he was being followed.

Garth turned around and went after the dog.

"Good boy!" he declared.

As he ran, he studied the thousands of people running in the same direction, desperate to see the familiar bonnet.

"Hey! It's time to go back!" he yelled when he saw one of the college students.

That guy shouted to one of his buddies, and they both turned around.

"Thanks!" the guy screamed over the noise.

Garth followed the growing crowd of people as they headed into the blue sparks. Some seemed hesitant to enter the electrical wall of energy, which now stretched about fifty feet above the fence line, but most ended up going in.

Now everyone could see the outline of the super collider. The blue light traced the curve on the ground, and neatly drew a circular shape between the town of Sedalia and the Hogback. It looked like a city-sized plate lying on the earth. Anyone looking from the fields of parked cars would have to realize they were on the wrong side of the dinner plate.

"Lydia!" he shouted.

Garth stopped before he reached the blue energy.

Masses of frightened people shoved by, crossed the downed fence, and ran into the field beyond.

Some soldiers parked Humvees over in the field, but they seemed like ants about to be overwhelmed by a flood.

"Lydia?"

Big Mac was gone. The students were gone. Everyone was crossing to the safety of the fence.

He couldn't go back yet.

The crackling sounds of the blue energy continued to surge, and he imagined he was risking his life by waiting for another second, but he couldn't cross the fence until he had found his friend.

Search for Nuclear, Astrophysical, and Kronometric Extremes (SNAKE). Red Mesa, Colorado

Faith was trapped in the control room, unable to do anything but watch.

The action at Sedalia was hard to follow. At the start, a lone soldier ran his pickup truck through the fence and used an American flag to wave people to him. Then a man in a black semi-truck cut down the fence longways, which started a stampede toward the safe side.

By the time the blue energy wave was a hundred feet tall on the video monitor, Faith's fingertips were crackling with the same blue sparks.

The control room came alive with sparkling lights, making her feel like the lone dancer on a disco floor. Dr. Johnson remained fixated on the screen, while the soldiers at the door seemed reluctant to move.

"I think this is going to be amazing, Faith," Dr. Johnson said breathlessly. "We've run this scenario a hundred thousand times on a Cray supercomputer, and each one was different. There is no precedent. No formula. No guide-post. But there will be, once we reach the other side. A new era of science, and for humanity."

"Go fuck yourself," she deadpanned. Billions of people were slated to die because of him.

Dr. Johnson laughed and slapped his paunch with both hands. "They never should have put a woman in charge of this collider. You can't make the hard decisions."

Blue energy burst out of a nearby control board like a fire hydrant gone wild.

Faith picked up a hardbound technical manual.

What the hell.

She quietly rose from her chair and sidled over to Dr. Johnson. The blue wall of dark energy bubbled out of the ground on two panels of the video monitor. A line crossed the lake in one frame, and it ran down a highway around Sedalia in the other. The third frame, showing the Four Arrows box, now, ironically, had no blue energy in it. The link to the box was finally off...

"Something's happening," he said with awe.

"Damn right it is."

She'd taken years of self-defense training, and had kept herself in shape so she would never become a victim. She had no control over the scientists hiding secret projects behind her back, but she retained full control over this moment.

She swung the hardbound book in a smooth arc, so it impacted squarely on the bridge of his nose.

"Oww!" he cried out.

"That's for Bob, you asshole."

"N-no!" he screamed.

She set up for another strike.

He stepped sideways to avoid it, but she used that

confused moment to push him into the wild stream of energy burning through the console. She had no idea what would happen when he touched it, but at the very least he was going to smash into the equipment.

He fell where she aimed him, and as soon as he touched the electricity, he disappeared.

"Oh, fuck!" she yelped.

She dropped the book and looked to the guards at the door, but they weren't there.

At least I did one good thing today.

More sparks emerged from other pieces of the control room, and it became a five-alarm fire of blue energy.

Faith fell to the floor.

Sedalia, CO

Buck ripped a hole in the fence a mile wide, and he felt damned good about it.

This is not going to be another Highway of Death.

When he reached a concrete outbuilding, he decided to turn around and go back. The soldiers in Humvees caught up with him, but there were so many cars surging onto the field that they must have figured there was no point in stopping him. They got out and waved people inside the fence like they should have been doing in the first place.

Fortunately, the people farther down the highway were paying attention to him and the light show now. Once they realized so many people were crossing the roadway, and once they saw him cutting down the fence, people didn't wait. Cars, trucks, and everything in between stormed the fence and got into the safe zone.

Buck chuckled, thinking about that Army dude waving

his American flag. He might have started the trickle, but Buck had used his Marine skills to put him to shame.

Buck smash!

After his few seconds of celebration, he put Lorraine in gear and headed to where he had last seen Garth. On the way back, he had to contend with the torrent of people coming through the smashed fence.

"Come on, let me sneak through here." He wove through the traffic and dodged the people until he got to where he'd started.

The blue electrical energy field was now as tall as a building, and it created a miles-long wall, like a tidal wave about to crest. The soldier with the flag was just inside the strange wall, still waving people through it.

Smart bastard. Showing people it's safe.

He had a grudging respect for the Army guy, but that was short-circuited when he finally saw Garth in the center of the crowd. Unlike everyone else, he stood still, as if looking around for something.

Buck worked the gears to get over to him, but there was a lot of foot traffic.

He hit the horn in short squawks to get his son's attention.

"Get out of there!"

In an instant, the entire wall of energy doubled in intensity. The land beyond the parked cars on his right shimmered like a desert mirage.

The beam sparked again, making the whole virtual wall of energy wobble.

His head felt woozy, and he had a suspicion about what was coming.

"Garth! Run!"

He was still a football field away, but he was fairly

certain a Golden Retriever and a girl in a bonnet ran up behind Garth.

Buck's vision blurred.

At the last possible moment, the kids locked hands, made sure the dog was with them, and ran for the blue light.

Then the whole world went blue.

TWENTY-SIX

Search for Nuclear, Astrophysical, and Krono-metric Extremes (SNAKE). Red Mesa, Colorado

"They're all gone, Faith. Every scientist who came with Dr. Johnson when he teleported or whatever from CERN disappeared when the blue light collapsed the time anomaly."

Faith stood at the glassless window in her old office.

"Thanks, Bob. I think they went back where they came from when the dark energy link was shut off. It serves them right for nuking their twins in CERN."

"Sheesh. You think that's what happened?"

She couldn't take her eyes off the new landscape outside.

"I saw Johnson get sucked into the blue energy myself. He simply vanished when he touched it. I tried to get away from it too, but eventually, there was too much."

"You made contact with it?"

"Yes," she said dryly. "We all did."

"It didn't take you away," he said matter-of-factly.

"No, the transplants were special. I think he had some

kind of anti-dark-matter charge like he didn't belong here. This reality couldn't handle two of him."

They shared a chuckle.

Faith turned his way, sounding less enthusiastic. "I tried calling my sister, but there isn't a network signal. It's like there's nothing out there. Boy, Benny's going to be pissed. He knows everything, like I promised, but there are no more newspapers."

"I'm sorry," he said. "Really, I mean that. I'm sorry a hundred times over for my role in all this."

She wasn't ready to forgive him.

"Do you think people can change?"

Bob flashed a fraction of his smile. "I certainly have."

"No, I don't mean this to be about us. You are still the jerk who wrote that stupid neutrino joke on the conference room table. Your hands are dirty from all this." She spoke with a little less snark. "Though I will admit ... you aren't even close to Dr. Johnson when it comes to credentials in the field of asshattery."

"I had no idea he was like that," he said in a contrite voice.

She gestured out the window. Sedalia was several miles away on the plains beyond the Hogback. The buildings and cars in and near the town glistened in the sunshine, providing a visible landmark for her. "He wanted to kill all those people. I'm not sure how they did it, but the people fought back. They weren't the sheep he thought they were, and boy, am I glad about it!"

"And what about the rest of it?" He swept his arm across her view.

The city of Denver had vanished, and the high plains of eastern Colorado were gone. There was now a giant blue sea with several small, tropical islands dotted along the near shore.

"If there are still people out there, they will have no choice but to change. I have a feeling our experiment did more than return this supercollider to a normal place in time. To keep us as we were, it had to destroy the rest of the world."

"No, you can't think of it like that. The rest of the world was going to die anyway. We managed to find the one place where the experiment was successful. And thanks to people like you, and those who broke the fences along our perimeter, humanity has a chance to survive what would have been sure death."

Faith looked at her ex with a newfound sense of gratitude. There was a good person somewhere down deep inside. Her question about change hadn't been meant for him, however, but for her.

The old Faith might have seen Bob in a new light and decided the worldwide calamity was reason enough to get back together with him. Countless books, movies, and television shows had ingrained the notion to the point it was almost automatic in her psyche. But she remembered being in that blue light. In those few seconds, she had seen countless possibilities for the new world, and had imagined herself thriving and surviving in them. Nothing in her visions suggested settling for a man like him was the path to a happily ever after.

"Thanks, Bob. It means a lot to hear you say that."

"I'm trying."

"I know." She chuckled. "Now, let's go get the others and show them how much work we have ahead of us."

The Four Arrows experiment was finally over.

The experiment called humanity was starting from scratch.

Somewhere at sea

"Destiny, wake up!"

She'd been dreaming about a forest fire and woke up with a pounding heart and a nose searching for smoke.

"Zandre? Are we on fire?"

"What? No. Look up there."

She sat up and saw the blue light streaking through the nighttime sky out of the northeast.

The ship was full of Sydney Harbor people and their families, so she and Zandre had to sleep on the deck. Since the lingering animosity from when they had left her at the fire still drove her nightmares, she didn't mind keeping her distance from them.

"I saw this light four days ago," Zandre whispered. "It kicked off all of our problems."

"Is this the end of it?" Dez asked, desperate to catch her breath.

The light moved fast, like a rogue wave in the air. It had been halfway across the sky when she woke up, and now it blazed off toward the horizon while she still blinked the sleep from her eyes.

Faith!

She pulled out her phone and tried to dial her sister, but there was no signal. That could have been because they were far from shore—

A claxon blared from the bridge.

"Collision! Collision! Brace yourselves!"

She'd been looking at the pretty lights in the sky, so she'd missed what was going on at the water's surface. Land

237

was a few hundred meters ahead. It was a black silhouette against the backdrop of starry sky, but it was there. White froth provided a clue about the rocky shore.

The engines roared, and the deck rumbled with it. The ship slowed as the captain fought to keep her from ramming land.

"Hang on, Dez," Zandre said dumbly.

She held her breath as the ship slowed.

Several crates of cargo shifted on the deck, pushing her sideways toward the railing.

"Bloody hell!"

The deck shuddered with the engine strain, but they were almost stopped.

"A little more," Zandre whispered.

For a couple of seconds, they were in between forward and reverse, and it felt like an eternity. Then the engines started them backing up.

More cargo shifted, but Dez didn't care.

"The bastard did it," she said joyously. "We're safe."

She let out a long sigh when it was certain they'd be all right.

"Phew! That would have ended our trip before we got started."

Zandre patted her on the back. "I couldn't have said it better, mate."

A few minutes later, the pair entered the bridge because she wanted to know if they'd heard anything on the short-wave about the blue streak in the sky.

"Ah, you two are all right. We wondered about you sleeping on the deck. Things shift from time to time."

Dez was almost touched.

"Can you tell us what happened?" she asked. "Can we still get to America?"

The captain looked at her with uncertainty in his eyes. "I can't say. We're off the charts right now."

"What does that mean?" Zandre inquired.

The captain pointed at a digital radar screen. "This just updated. The shoreline doesn't belong here. We are in the middle of the Coral Sea, and there isn't supposed to be land for five hundred kilometers in any direction. Now we have this."

She wasn't a nautical person, but it looked like the screen showed a long piece of land going from one side of the readout to the other. It was as if they'd pulled up next to a continent.

"Are we at Papua New Guinea?" Zandre asked.

"Nope, not unless we moved a thousand kilometers in the last five minutes."

She and Zandre exchanged glances.

Destiny was crestfallen. "Captain, I told you we had to hurry. I think...maybe...we can take our time now, because we missed our chance."

"The engines are fine. We can keep going once we get around this blockage."

She looked again at the radar screen. "You can try, but I think you'll find this isn't New Guinea. At least, not in the modern era."

"Whatever does that mean?" the captain asked with impatience.

"It means we've watched animals come back from the past. We've watched land reclaim itself by blinking out modern structures, like the Opera House, or the shoreline by the docks. My sister was telling the truth when she said the only place to truly be safe was SNAKE. Now we're stuck in the reclaimed world, along with all the treasures dredged up from the past."

"So we got mixed up," the captain went on. "I think this big landmass might be Australia again. It makes a little sense, right?"

"Are the stars correct? Can you use them as a guide?" she asked. "I saw the Southern Cross as clear as could be just now. It hasn't moved, as far as I can tell."

The captain looked out a side window. "Yep, still there. I checked it not long ago, too. I do it from time to time on night watch, since it is easy to tip off when I get tired. That's good thinking, young lady. It proves we haven't moved."

"So what does it tell us?" Zandre asked. "The land moved to us?"

She was unwilling to let one more challenge bring her down, so she laughed to lighten the mood. "I guess we're going to have to wait until the sun rises to see what we've got, right, mates? Who knows, we might already be sitting off the coast of California. Wouldn't that be a cracking good time?"

She made a promise she didn't intend to break.

I'll make it to you, sis, no matter what's out there.

Red Mesa, CO

"Am I going to stay with you now, Garth?" Lydia sat next to him on a log as he tended a small fire.

"I think so. The blue sparks are gone and the whole planet has changed, but you and Connie are still here. That makes sense, right, Dad?"

His father sat across the fire. "I'm calling this done. No one is taking my woman away from me."

Garth bumped Lydia. "I'd like to keep mine, too."

"Hmf," Lydia blurted. "Don't I get a choice in this?"

She acted stern, but she was terrible at it. She constantly had to squelch her giggles.

"Oh, sure, if you can find anyone willing to ride cross-country with you, I'll happily let you go with them." Garth pointed to the crowd of survivors around them. "You said you are from Wyoming, right?"

"Indiana. We were going to Wyoming, but I don't want to go there," she said quickly, as if he might put her on a bus at that moment.

He softened. "I'm kidding. I said I'd try to get you home, and I stand by the statement, but I don't want you to go back. I've, uh, had fun with you."

Out of the blue, she leaned over and kissed him briefly.

"I agree to a courtship!"

Garth's emotions were a whirlpool. He hadn't exactly come out and asked her in those terms, but once the surprise was over, he realized he was happy she had spelled it out for him.

He looked at his dad, wondering if he needed his approval, but it seemed silly after all that had happened.

Buck winked at him.

"Garth, do you think we could start a homestead out there?" She pointed to the shoreline across the new body of water.

His heart did a backflip.

"I, uh..." he stuttered.

"One thing at a time, kids," Buck said with a laugh. "First, let's talk about finding a preacher. Then we'll start building cities."

Nice save, Dad.

He wanted everything with Lydia, but he also wanted to take it slow. It looked like the fast-paced world was gone, at least for a while by the looks of things, so there was plenty of time.

"Dad, do you think we can live out there? What do you think we'll find?"

The cars that had been parked on the far side of the highway were gone, as was much of the pavement of the road. Now, the highway was beachfront property at the edge of a large ocean.

"I have no idea. We saw Lake Bonneville fill up with water like it was eons ago, so maybe this used to be a giant lake sometime in the past."

They all agreed that the blue light had reverted things back to how they had been in the past, except for the people and things inside the SNAKE supercollider ring. It had happened exactly as Mr. Shinano and Doctor Sinclair had warned.

As to what was out there, they could only guess, based on what they could see.

Garth spoke quietly. "I could definitely live on the beach."

He spun around to look at the other big change. The hills and pine forest above their location still looked like the foothills of the Rocky Mountains, but now the mountains in the background seemed twice as tall as they had been before. If the inland ocean was supposed to be what that area looked like in the past, it made sense that the mountains now looked like they had at a far distant time in history.

Buck spoke before he could say what was on his mind. "Nobody's going anywhere until we talk to someone at SNAKE. We want to make sure the changes are over, and that if we step outside the circle, we aren't going to be sent into the past ourselves."

Garth took Lydia's hand, which made them both start to laugh.

Slow and steady.

"I already have all I need right here."

Buck's Rock

"Aww." Connie swooned at Garth's profession of love. "You two make such a cute couple. I'm glad we all made it together."

Buck read her emotions and wanted to steer her away from the ditch that was her lost son.

"The old America is gone," he said with resolve, "so I'm free to start renaming things. I'm going to call this place Buck's Rock."

He tapped a large sandstone outcropping, which was where they had gone after getting clear of the blue light. Since there were thousands of people in the fields near Sedalia, he and his friends had moved their vehicles right up against the Hogback. It gave them a degree of privacy while they planned what to do next.

"You can't claim rocks." Connie laughed.

"Oh, yes I can. This is a new land, and there is no law. No busybodies at the government labeling office. We can call things whatever we want."

"I call that!" Garth pointed to the water. "I'm going to call it the Lydian Ocean."

Lydia gave him a strange look.

"What? Too soon?"

"You named a whole ocean after me? No one has ever done anything close to that. Not even my pa would have done such a thing."

Garth seemed embarrassed. "Well, it's not official. Not really..."

"I'm good with that, son," Buck said proudly. He wanted Garth to take things seriously, but there was also an element of fun that existed with life. If what he saw outside the collider ring had happened all over Earth, there whole way of life had changed forever. There was plenty of time to be serious later.

There would be no more fuel.

No more pre-packaged food.

No more help.

He wondered how many doctors had been inside the perimeter. How many police. How many criminals. What was the balance of men and women? The Marine in him started a ledger of supplies and what they would need to scrounge for daily survival.

And we've got to have a lot of kids.

Buck glanced at Connie. She gave him a look, then stood and walked away from the fire.

"I'll be right back," he said to Garth and the others. Evelyn, Clarence, and Mel Tinker sat at the fire too. He figured there was no point in using their CB handles because there were no more highways.

After a short jog, he caught up with his cowgirl friend.

"Howdy, partner," she drawled.

He knew what was on her mind.

"Hey, I'm getting ready to go back down to the crowd and look around. Will you go with me? I want to look for your son."

"Buck—"

"No, I want to, okay? I said I would, and I meant it. We can do this."

He'd been coming to terms with why he had pushed so

hard to destroy the fence. It wasn't only to prove a point over the Army guy, although that made a convenient excuse. His real reason had to do with wanting to rescue every human he possibly could, so he could prove he had tried with all his soul to find her missing son. And, because so few people had made it relative to the whole country, he was prepared to deal with his failure.

"It's not that. I think I saw my son when we came in."

He wasn't sure if she was serious.

"It's true." She poked him in the side. "At least, I hope it is."

"Well, uh, let's go get him. Where is he?"

"This sounds insane, but I thought he was there when you drove through the fence the first time. The soldier waving the American flag looked like him, but I didn't think about it until after I had those kids out of your trailer. It got totally crazy for a few minutes, and when I finally got around to looking for him, I thought I saw him disappear in the blue electricity. I passed out when it happened, and he wasn't there when I came around."

They'd all fainted when the final pulse shot out of the ground.

He gave her a hug, not sure he totally believed her, but ready to back her up no matter what. "The Army guy?"

She smacked him harder.

"I just want him back," she said sadly.

"We'll eat and then go, okay? We'll spend all day if we have to. Talk to every person here."

He looked into her teary green eyes and took the conversation in a new direction.

"I'm glad you didn't fade out of existence. When I drove over that fence, all I thought about was you and Garth getting sucked away by the blue light." He chuckled. "Of course, it shouldn't surprise you that it was Garth who gave me the heart attack. He and Lydia almost didn't make it back."

"Thank God for Mac, right?"

"Amen."

The pup had gone out and brought back his son. He was now convinced that the dog was much smarter than he was.

They hugged. Then, for much too brief a time, they kissed.

"Shall we go back to the family?" he asked.

"I like the sound of that."

"That reminds me, there's something I've been meaning to ask you."

His guts quivered. He'd only known her for a little over four days, but everything had changed. It appeared as if all of existence on Earth was now different. Connie was an anchor to the old world, but also a sail to guide him into the new. There was nothing that could make him think otherwise about her.

"I can't let my son marry his girl before I do..."

Formerly Sedalia, CO

Phil was thrilled to still be in Colorado. After the blue light had washed over him and all the people on the fence line, he had assumed he would be beamed back to Switzerland or spat out of existence. The only thing that had kept him from running out of the wall of blue at the last moment was a young boy, a strangely dressed girl, and their shaggy dog.

They ran by him as the blast knocked him on his ass.

When he woke up, the people and cars across the street were gone.

The soldiers didn't bother him. They had regrouped, and were offering water and bits of food to the survivors as if the battle was over. He was going to get to the bottom of who they were, and how a ghost unit like the 130th could even exist here, but once he got to his feet, he had another mission on his mind.

"That lady looked familiar..."

The first truck through the fence had had a woman who was the spitting image of his mom. She was young, like the year he had last seen her, so it couldn't have been her. However, the mere act of seeing the lookalike stirred feelings of loss and guilt he needed to stomp out. He could only do that by finding the woman.

He saw the truck right away. The bug-covered mess of a semi was easy to spot, even in a field filled with hundreds of cars and thousands of people. However, being a lieutenant colonel worked against him. It took him a long time to get across the makeshift camp because everyone saw him as a person in charge.

It was lunchtime before he got to the far side of the crowd. During his delay, the trucker had re-attached his trailer and driven it and two other trucks farther across the field, all the way to the rocky outcrop before the start of the hills.

I should have had Grafton drop me off.

His partner had taken the pickup truck to go find the other members of Task Force Blue 7.

He recognized the over-the-road driver the second he came around the back of the trailer. The guy sat at a cooking fire along with a small group of friends. The two young people he had seen in the street were there with them. Even the dog was there. The Golden Retriever cocked its head as he neared.

The redhead was also seated at the fire, as he suspected, but she had her back to him. The woman wore blue jeans and a white shirt and a fancy belt with lots of bling, as his cowgirl mother would have called it.

Might be a coincidence.

"Excuse me. I don't want any trouble," he called.

The truck driver was the first out of his seat. "Can we help you, soldier?" He wore a hideous Hawaiian shirt, but he stood tall in front of his people as if to protect them. Probably military.

The man waved him in. "Want a bite to eat? We're cooking rabbit. I picked it up on the California-Nevada border when the world went to shit, and I've been saving it for a special occasion."

"Nevada, you say?" That was where Mom had gone missing.

Another weird coincidence.

"Yeah, shot it in the woods. Hell, I have a truck full of chili, but we can't let anything go to waste now, can we?"

"No, I guess not. Thanks for the offer, but I can't stay. I actually came up here for the dumbest reason you've ever heard. When you broke through the first fence, I saw a woman in your passenger seat who looked a lot like someone who went missing a few years back. I figured it was a long shot, but I had to know for sure."

The man lit up with excitement. "I recognize you! The Army guy! That was some nice work you did at the fence line. Too bad you needed a Marine to come in and show you how to finish it."

It had to be a devil dog.

Phil let his guard down a bit. "Next time, you drive the

little truck, and I'll take the big one. Good work yourself. You saved most of the people on this field."

"It was a team effort," Hawaiian Shirt said with real humility. Then, in a weird change of attitude, he backed up to the woman and put a hand on her shoulder. She still hadn't turned around.

The Marine spoke in a low voice. "Talk about luck. We were about to search for you for the same reason."

His pulse quickened as tumblers fell in the lock inside his heart.

"Is that your passenger?" Phil pointed to the woman.

"Can I tell her who's asking?"

The lady pulled at the Marine's hand to get his attention. Almost too low to hear, the woman spoke.

The Marine looked at her in surprise. "You can tell by his voice?" He peered at Phil like he'd just beamed down from an alien ship.

"Are you Phil Stanwick, by chance?"

There was no possible way anyone could know who he was. He still had Sargent on the name tape of his borrowed uniform. Phil bit his lip to control the turbulent emotions he'd been holding in for the past seventeen years.

He straightened. "I'm Lieutenant Colonel Philip Stanwick, 3rd Battalion, 75th Ranger Regiment, United States Army."

The Marine gave him a proper salute, then spoke to the woman. "Connie, you were right, of course. You can finally stop trying to call your boy."

When the woman stood up and turned around, he saw his mom as she had been at the time of her disappearance. The exact style of long red hair. The same green eyes. Even the same style of clothing. It couldn't be anyone else.

"I don't believe it," he said, shocked. "Mom?"

The Golden Retriever ran over to Phil and got up on his hind legs to unleash a massive canine hug. The big dog made him stumble a few steps back and he suffered a barrage of dog kisses, but he managed to hold his ground.

"Big Mac knows family," his long-lost mother said through a sea of tears.

The Marine came forward with his hand out. "Welcome home. I'm Buck."

To Be Continued in End Days, Book 5?

If you liked this book, please leave a review. This is a new series, so the only way I can decide whether to commit more time to it is by getting feedback from you, the readers. Your opinion matters to me. Continue or not? I have only so much time to craft new stories. Help me invest that time wisely. Plus, reviews buoy my spirits and stoke the fires of creativity.

Don't stop now! Keep turning the pages as there's a little more insight and such from the authors.

COPYRIGHT

AUTHOR NOTES – E.E. ISHERWOOD

Written February 27, 2019

Is *End Days* over?

Craig and I set out to write exactly four novels in this series. Over the course of 1200 pages we've kicked apart the supports of civilization, ripped out all the wiring, and burned whatever was left. Except for a small, 300-square-mile circular parcel of land in what used to be Colorado, the world we know and love is completely gone.

So, what comes next for our heroes?

Buck and his friends cook rabbit while gazing out on a prehistoric world. They are surrounded by a few thousand survivors. Are there enough doctors? Enough plumbers? Enough soldiers? If they manage to survive and tame the new wilderness, are there even enough people to re-populate the world?

And don't forget Dez. She got a late start on her way to SNAKE and fell short of her goal. However, she proves not everyone disappeared when the dark energy bubble popped. How many others are out there? And from what eras?

Didn't Mr. Shinano hint there were two legitimate places on earth to get safe? What if someone is still toying with the dark energy inside the earth? Is it possible to make things even worse? Humans always find a way to mess things up, it seems...

If this sounds like a promotion for book five, well, maybe it is.

If you'll indulge a degree of self-promotion, the surest way to ensure more books will be written in this series is to explore our other titles. That gives us a little scratch to buy more typewriter ink ribbons and also gives *End Days* time to build up a bigger audience, so book 5 becomes financially viable.

Buy Craig's books first—he invited me into his house to write with him—but then I hope you'll check out my back catalog, too. I'll be creating new content this summer, though as of this writing I'm not sure what it will be called. Post-Apocalyptic goodness is all I can guarantee right now.

You can also check out my seven-book series, *Since the Sirens*. The first book is free, so there is no risk. Once you get in and learn about my teen hero and the grandma he saves from the plague, I hope you'll find it as engaging of a journey as *End Days*.

I even put a few little Easter eggs in *End Days*, linking this world back to *Since the Sirens*. When you are dealing with a reality-twisting supercollider, perhaps things bleed over from one universe to the next?

Reviews help our series grow, so please leave a review for this one. Tell your friends about us. Ask your library to stock our titles. It is amazing to have your feedback and support, and it really does help our careers.

As the popularity of all our books grow, we are able to continue writing in universes like *End Days*. There is more story there, to be sure, so book five might one day get the green light.

Speaking of stories, I'm always fascinated by coincidences when I write my books. *Begin Again* had a big one.

About forty years ago, my father gave me one of the glue-together models he made when he was a kid. Most of the planes are missing, and many of the tiny pieces broke off long ago, but I've kept it on my shelf all these years because it belonged to him.

That model was the USS *Wasp*, which is the ship Buck and Connie see on the side of the road. I could have chosen any named ship from the past five-hundred years, but I picked that one because of the model.

A day or two after I wrote that chapter this past March, I learned a research vessel found the wreck of the USS *Wasp* where it was sunk in World War II.

How many stars had to line up for that to work out with such symmetry?

As I look out my Missouri window today, I see the sunshine and warmth of springtime finally kicking into high gear. As the leaves begin to fill in on the trees, it signals a renewal of the world. I imagine Buck, Garth, Connie, and Lydia are feeling the same way as they *Begin Again*.

Thank you for spending your time in their universe.

And thank you Craig for giving me this wonderful opportunity.

Once you've signed up for Craig's **newsletter**, I would be thrilled to have you also join **mine**.

That's all the time I have. The next book calls to me!

AUTHOR NOTES - CRAIG MARTELLE

Written April 16, 2019

You are still reading! Thank you so much. It doesn't get much better than that.

At this point, the story completed its initial arc. This will probably be the end of the series unless the fan outcry is great enough. If you need more Buck, Connie, Garth, and Lydia, what would the future look like? So much potential for a next phase, how would they survive and knowing them as you do, how would they help the world come back to itself because you know there is no way they wouldn't stretch out a helping hand?

Spring has come early to the Alaskan interior! While there are areas in the lower 48 that just got snow, we've had a mild and welcoming spring. Phyllis the Arctic Dog and I are getting plenty of time in the woods behind our house.

She found a ptarmigan underneath a fallen tree and chased it. She has little hope of ever catching one of our state birds. I used to yell at her not to chase them, but she gets some exercise and the ptarmigan never fly very far. They aren't afraid of her. She'll be 12 this year and has slowed down a bit.

We are always on the lookout for moose, though. Getting between a cow and a calf can be deadly. More people die in Alaska each year from moose attacks than from bears. A full-grown cow could be a thousand pounds. It doesn't take much for them to hurt one of us fragile humans.

I have a major fishing trip coming in June. My dad will be here for his 83rd birthday. We're going fishing down on the Kenai Peninsula – a couple charters on the ocean out of Homer and a couple days fishing the Kenai River. We'll be driving my truck down – it'll be time well spent with my dad. I only get to see him a couple times a year. He still has plenty of energy, but the years are passing. Don't miss these chances.

That's it, now. I'm off to keep writing and working with my co-authors to bring these incredible stories to you.

Peace, fellow humans.

If you liked the story, please write a short review for me on Amazon. I greatly appreciate any kind words, and even one or two sentences go a long way. The number of reviews an ebook receives greatly improves how well an ebook does on Amazon.

If you liked this story, you might like some of my other books. You can join my mailing list by dropping by my website **www.craigmartelle.com** where you'll always be the first to hear when I put my books on sale. Or if you have any comments, shoot me a note at craig@craigmartelle.com. I am always happy to hear from people who've read my work. I try to answer every email I receive.

Amazon – www.amazon.com/author/craigmartelle

BookBub – https://www.bookbub.com/authors/craig-martelle

Facebook – www.facebook.com/authorcraigmartelle

My web page – www.craigmartelle.com

E.E. ISHERWOOD'S OTHER BOOKS

End Days (co-written with Craig Martelle) – a post-apocalyptic adventure

Sirens of the Zombie Apocalypse – What if the only people immune are those over 100? A teen boy must keep his great-grandma alive to find the cure for the zombie plague.

Eternal Apocalypse – Set seventy years after the zombies came, a group of survivors manipulates aging to endure their time in survival bunkers, but it all falls apart when a young girl feels sunlight for the first time.

Amazon – **amazon.com/author/eeisherwood**

Facebook – **www.facebook.com/sincethesirens**

My web page – **www.sincethesirens.com**

CRAIG MARTELLE'S OTHER BOOKS

(LISTED BY SERIES) (# - AVAILABLE IN AUDIO, TOO)

Terry Henry Walton Chronicles (# co-written with Michael Anderle) – a post-apocalyptic paranormal adventure

Gateway to the Universe (# co-written with Justin Sloan & Michael Anderle) – this book transitions the characters from the Terry Henry Walton Chronicles to The Bad Company

The Bad Company (# co-written with Michael Anderle) – a military science fiction space opera

End Times Alaska (#) – a Permuted Press publication – a post-apocalyptic survivalist adventure

The Free Trader – a Young Adult Science Fiction Action Adventure

Cygnus Space Opera – # A Young Adult Space Opera (set in the Free Trader universe)

Darklanding (co-written with Scott Moon) – a Space Western

Judge, Jury, & Executioner – # a space opera adventure legal thriller

Rick Banik – # Spy & Terrorism Action Adventure

Become a Successful Indie Author – a non-fiction work

Metamorphosis Alpha – stories from the world's first science fiction RPG

The Expanding Universe – science fiction anthologies

Shadow Vanguard – a Tom Dublin series

Enemy of my Enemy (co-written with Tim Marquitz) – A galactic alien military space opera

Superdreadnought (co-written with Tim Marquitz) – an AI military space opera

Metal Legion (co-written with Caleb Wachter) – a galactic military sci-fi with mechs

End Days (co-written with E.E. Isherwood) – a post-apocalyptic adventure

Mystically Engineered (co-written with Valerie Emerson) – dragons in space

Monster Case Files (co-written with Kathryn Hearst) – a young-adult cozy mystery series

Nightwalker (a Frank Roderus series) – a post-apocalyptic survival adventure

Made in United States
Troutdale, OR
05/11/2024

19752512R00156